ANGELS

FRANK DUMOND

ISBN: 979-8-89075-807-1

Contents

Chapter 1: The Beginning of Life

In the boundless expanse of the cosmos, where galaxies swirled in harmonious choreography, an extraordinary dimension known as the heavens existed. This ethereal realm was the sanctum of celestial beings whose purpose was to behold the marvels of creation. Amidst these divine entities, one shone with unrivaled brilliance – God.

God, the ultimate and supreme being, possessed limitless wisdom and boundless power. With but a thought, galaxies burst forth, stars ignited the void, and planets emerged from the void. Yet, God aspired to do more than the mere act of creation. The heavens themselves hungered for a spectacle that would enrapture their eternal existence.

Deep within God's unfathomable mind, a grand design began to form. A design that would give birth to a world, sculpted to perfection, teeming with life, and inhabited by beings endowed with free will, capable of both profound love and profound darkness. This world would come to be known as Earth, a stage for a grand cosmic drama.

To inaugurate this spectacle, God extended a hand through the fabric of time and space, stirring anticipation within the heavens. In the blink of an eye, matter and energy condensed, birthing a swirling tempest of fire and light. From this primal chaos, galaxies took form, stars were born, and planets were scattered across the cosmos.

Among these celestial bodies, Earth emerged—a sapphire jewel adrift in the boundless sea of the cosmos. God beheld this creation, with its expansive oceans and towering peaks, its verdant forests and scorching deserts. It was a canvas of boundless potential, ready to be painted with life.

And so, God's focus shifted to Earth's inhabitants, the beings destined to infuse life and vitality into this precious world. With meticulous care, God crafted the first of humanity, Adam and Eve. Born from the very essence of their Creator, they carried the divine spark within them.

Adam and Eve were perfection incarnate, reflecting the splendor and love of their maker. They possessed intellect, compassion, and the capacity for growth. God placed them within a bountiful garden known as Eden, where they would flourish and prosper. In this paradise, the celestial beings of the heavens are observed with rapt attention, mesmerized by the unfolding drama.

As Adam and Eve explored their newfound abode, the heavens watched with awe and delight. Every caress of the breeze and every subtle shift of the seasons showcased God's omnipotence and creativity. The celestial beings reveled in these earthly wonders, for they were the true audience of this cosmic spectacle.

However, amidst Eden's splendors, a trace of unease crept through the heavens. God, in His infinite wisdom, had endowed Adam and Eve with free will. With this gift came the potential for choice, both virtuous and malevolent. And so, in the ethereal realms above, whispers of uncertainty stirred.

God, ever watchful, recognized the lingering apprehension among the divine beings. He acknowledged their concerns but remained steadfast in His decision not to impose fear and control. Instead, God believed in the potential of love and the growth that could arise from autonomous choices, even if it entailed venturing into perilous terrain.

The Genesis, the Big Bang, Creation, all of it is just one big game of chess. It is played by Jesus and Lucifer with humans as pawns.

Sometimes people raise questions that philosophers and theologians have been debating since the beginning of time there are some questions, we don't have answers to, perhaps because we are not supposed to know 'everything', be in on every little divine joke, completely and God has only revealed in part what he ultimately will reveal to us completely on that day (of Judgement) when Jesus will slap his thigh and laugh so hard that he will start shedding tears, "Did you figure out? You Monkeys?"

"What?"

"This I all a farce, a ceramic dildo up the human beings' asses."

"What?"

"Why else would He let Palestine be devoured like it is?"

Silence

"Because He created this shit hole for His entertainment, nothing more, nothing less.

"Why was Azazel (Lucifer) a high-ranking angel? When God knew what He would do? You know, predestination, pre-knowledge…?"

"Why?"

"To have fun with us."

"What rubbish?"

"Fair trade… Explain the fucking Jews to me, the crème de la crème of Earth? Those people have only caused mischief and killed messengers. And He makes them the chosen people, the Bani Israel, parts the sea and what not for them?"

"Er…"

"What do they do in return?"

"Revolt?"

"Why?"

"I dunno, It's their primal instinct to…"

"Enough with the false reasoning… He wants to have fun and the conflicts that claim billions of lives are mere entertainment for him; mothers wailing upon the corpse of their charred children's bodies, eh, children dying of thirst and torture by the chosen ones?"

"Isn't that…?"

"Stop deluding yourself. You're nothing but a clown in a Pogo dress, if you can entertain Him, sure, if you can't, you get pushed to the other side, where heads are chopped off as He watches from high above."

Why Did God Create Humans

Why did God create human beings if He knew they would reject him and bring sin into the world well first of all it's not as if He did not know, He knew, God certainly knew when he fashioned Adam and Eve that men would fall, that sin would enter the world He knew that before he created Adam and Eve. When he created the angels we know the story of Lucifer; and how Lucifer came into being he was created as an angel sitting at the highest of God's angelic rank and yet God knew when he created Lucifer that Lucifer would want to embrace the worship that he was responsible for bringing back to God. He wanted that worship to be directed to him and so he fell along with a third of the angels that are now called demons and God knew that before he created and fashioned those angels.

A third of them fell, two-thirds of them remained loyal, and then after that, he created Adam and Eve knowing full well that they would indeed sin eat of the forbidden fruit, and fall in the same way that Lucifer fell, well now the question becomes why would he do that and the answer is that He has a purpose and he has a plan that plans and that purpose is referred to in Scripture years says from the beginning of the Bible Genesis to the end revelation – which, in retrospect is all hogwash – we have this unpacking of this plan of redemption this plan of salvation and just as God in Genesis creates the heavens and the earth in the book of Revelation He recreates the heavens in the earth out of the old. He creates a new and the books in between or the story of that journey of revealing to man His plan and His purpose for us and frankly, it's referred to in just those terms it is God as a plan. We think God has a purpose but he never in Scripture fully tells us what that plan and purpose is until the very last chapters of the last book of the Bible the book of Revelation. And if you read carefully, the element of divine divertissement is right there in front of you, where He speaks of a new heaven and a new earth where there will be no more death and no more sorrow and no more pain because all the former things are passed away and behold, He creates all new things. That is to overcomplicate things.

Well, we learn more about this in the book of Ephesians in Chapter 1, when it talks about Christ (a fictionalized character from the Bible, which isn't even real. We have obtained a theoretic, and a chimerical inheritance having been predestined here it is according to the purpose of Him – as He claims – who works all things according to the counsel of *His will* and there we have it boys and girls) so that we who were the first to hope in Christ were the first to cry.

All your sorry lives you've believed in stuff such as 'salvation' and believed in Him as a 'good' God; you were sealed with the promise of the Spirit (if I tell you who the Spirit is you will probably tear out your hair – it's all in the gospel of Barnabus and the Song of David.

"Who was the guarantee or deposit of our inheritance until we acquire possession of it to the praise of His glory?

"Now he talks to us about a plan of redemption that ends in the praise of His glory, His amusement ends with us receiving glorification without compunction."

"But that is a day in which we will receive the fullness of all that God has promised to us, until then there is a…"

"Wait, wait… Your gods are Amazon and Netflix, why the hell are you being so defensive? That is another mystery that shrouds the plan and the purpose of God."

"It's referred to again and again and again that God has a plan and God has a purpose now we've always liked to raise the question; what did God do since He is eternal, since he has no beginning, He has no end?

"My question is what did God do with His… We'll call it time, when there was no time what did He do before time began? What was God's plan and purpose for Lucifer and what about before he created the angels what about before He created Lucifer God existed then.

"Hence there's a mystery of the Godhead that we cannot comprehend we cannot understand. Now we get a little clue about this when…"

"But…"

"Hush. The Apostle Paul was whipped – with an inch of his life and there between the cities of Derbe and Lystra, he lies on the ground he has an out-of-body experience because he's been beaten to a pulp and he is transported just for a moment to see what that glory that God promises is? That's part of poor Paul's plan, what that glory looks like. Makes me laugh."

Marquis de Sade said, "God strung up His son like a side of veal. I shudder to think what he would do to me."

"But that comes from the filthiest man to ever have lived,"

"'*The Marquis*' said it, not *Benji Netanyahu*, the ass, a jester in the greater scheme of things."

"You talk nonsense."

"Yeah? And when he sees that as he is sent back into his body as he is sent back to earth, he is commanded by God not to try to share with anyone. Not to 'try and share', what was he Jesus or a twelve-year-old high schooler from the West?"

"What he saw, and there's a reason for that because no words would be able to describe in fullness what that glory looks like."

"Yeah yeah, whatever you wanna think to tolerate this dismal existence.

"God has shrouded that ultimate purpose, that ultimate plan he has shrouded it from us because we cannot possibly understand if we hear loud laughter coming down from the heavens, we'd become baffled. Forget it friend-o. We cannot possibly explain it, we cannot possibly elaborate on it, because it is too simple and yet too mighty, thanks to the false prophets, for any of us to understand. So yes, there is a plan there is a purpose and there is a reason why this omniscient God, this all-knowing, all-powerful, all-present God, all-bored God created individuals that he could play with.

"Why else would He smile when He knew we would betray Him? He knew that sin would enter the world, that He would allow it to enter, but as we read the facetious Bible from cover to cover the centerpiece of all that God wants us to know is that in time, in actual time, God is but a mass arrest magistrate and would become a man. Are you serious? You call that the Incarnation, that God would become a man and he would take upon himself the sins of all the people he plans to redeem and set free in the end anyway, and in that incarnation, we see we catch a glimpse of God's purpose to redeem fallen man from their sins to redeem us from our disobedience?

"So even those who take it in the bum go to heaven?"

"Heaven or whatever there is where all the dearly or not too dearly (Netanyahu) end up, and this is only to put us on a tangent, *'offer to us a gift of grace a gift of*

> *salvation and that gift of salvation is*

> *offered to all men everywhere and to*

> *those who receive him to them he gives*

"Really, who do you think you are? King Baldwin IV?"

"It can't be true."

"Would a mother burn her child, under any circumstances, other than being a bona fide psycho?"

"I don't think so…"

"Exactly and so ultimately the plan and purpose of God is to point people back to the Dark and not to the fictitious cross of Jesus Christ. I like the name I wonder who penned it?"

"You're wrong, this is because it is an act of self-sacrifice."

"Lovely."

"God reveals to us the great love that He has that even while we were yet sinners. As the first chapter of this cosmic drama neared its zenith, God made a solemn pledge. He assured the heavens that His love for humanity would transcend…."

"Gimme a break. What this is, is the face of chaos and darkness, a glimmer of hope would never persist in the clouds of the smoke that rises from the rubble of a bombed civilian shelter."

Long live Netanyahu and Emanuel Macron.

Little did they foresee that this narrative would encompass not only the peaks of human achievement but also the depths of human suffering—a tapestry woven by the choices and actions of every individual who would tread upon the Earth. As the first chapter drew to a close, heralding the dawn of a new era, the fate of humanity rested firmly in their own hands.

The heavens observed, poised to witness the ongoing drama, as God's quest for entertainment continued to unravel. Each subsequent chapter remained unwritten, and each twist of fate remained unforeseen, as the narrative of Earth and its inhabitants danced to the rhythm of their own free will. And so, the heavens remained captivated, eagerly awaiting their role as witnesses to the marvelous tapestry of life on Earth.

Adam and Eve awoke each morning to the lilting melodies of birdsong and the gentle caress of sunlight filtering through the leaves of fruit-laden trees. Every day was a celebration of nature's abundance.

Adam, a towering figure with eyes as deep as the cosmos and a benevolent smile, assumed the role of steward of the garden. He nurtured the plants, ensuring their vitality and providing sustenance for both himself and Eve. Meanwhile, Eve, with her radiant smile and flowing chestnut tresses, embarked on journeys into the heart of Eden, marveling at the rich tapestry of flora and fauna.

As they ventured deeper into the garden's embrace, they encountered an astounding variety of fruits—succulent apples, juicy strawberries, and plump grapes. These fruits not only nourished their bodies but also ignited their senses with wonder and delight. Adam and Eve reveled in the flavors and textures of each bite, rejoicing in the goodness of God's creation.

Amidst their explorations, Adam and Eve encountered creatures of every size and shape, living in harmony with one another. They shared a tranquil connection with these animals. Eve delighted in the gentle touch of a butterfly's wings against her skin, while Adam found joy in the playful antics of a family of monkeys swinging from the branches above.

As days turned to weeks and weeks to years, Adam and Eve continued to explore the wonders of Eden. Their love for one another deepened, forging an unbreakable bond. Their conversations overflowed with laughter and dreams of what lay beyond the garden's borders.

In their blissful existence, Adam and Eve engaged in dialogues with God, their divine Creator. During these precious moments, God imparted His wisdom and guidance, encouraging them to explore their surroundings and deepen their understanding of themselves and the world around them.

Yet, with time, a yearning stirred within their souls. Despite the utopia they inhabited, they could not suppress their curiosity about what lay beyond the confines of Eden. Adam envisioned scaling towering mountains and discovering hidden valleys, while Eve yearned to plumb the enigmatic depths of the vast ocean.

Sensing this restlessness, God listened attentively to their desires. He comprehended the need for growth and self-discovery and made a momentous decision—to bestow upon them a gift that would unlock their potential, allowing them to explore Earth's boundless expanse.

And so, as the chapter drew to a close, a new dawn approached. Unbeknownst to Adam and Eve, they stood on the precipice of a world teeming with limitless possibilities, where they would encounter the ecstasy of triumph and the agony of defeat. The stage remained set, and the cosmic drama continued to unfold, with the heavens watching in eager anticipation, ready to witness the next chapter in the odyssey of Adam and Eve.

Chapter 2: War of the Heavens

"Did you ever notice how in the Bible, whenever God needed to punish someone or make an example, or whenever God needed a killing, he sent an angel? Did you ever wonder what a creature like that must be like? A whole existence spent praising your God, but always with one wing dipped in blood. Would you ever really want to see an angel?" – **Det. Thomas Daggett**, *The Prophecy* 1995

"Do you know how you got that dent, in your top lip? Way back, before you were born, I told you a secret, then I put my finger there and I said "Shhhhh!" – **Gabriel**, *The Prophecy*, 1995[1]

I felt sickened by the terrible treatment meted out to an innocent and defenseless man as I strolled down the crowded city street. The first thing I wanted to do was ignore it and carry on walking, just like everyone else in the area. But I had to take action because my conscience wouldn't allow me.

The man, whose age could not have exceeded thirty, lay on the ground, his body trembling in terror and blood streaming from his face. Three young males surrounded him, laughing and mocking him as they kicked and punched him.

---

[1] ©Dimension Dimension Films; ©First Look Studios; ©NEO Motion Pictures; ©Overseas Film Company

I rushed in their direction, hatred, and rage pounding in my chest. I was baffled as to how these individuals could take pleasure in inflicting such agony and suffering on a defenseless victim.

"What's going on here, buddy?" Trying to seem confident, I yelled.

The men turned to confront me; rage twisted in their features. Even though they were bigger and stronger than I was, I couldn't watch this atrocity happen.

"Respect yourself, human," scoffed one of them.

As a human being, this is my business. Why are you treating him in this way? Pointing to the frail guy on the ground, I demanded.

One of them hissed, dragging every word, *"He owes us prominence, and we want it back."*

I turned to face the man, who was now attempting to drag himself free from his assailants. His clothing was ripped, his face injured, and it was obvious he was having financial difficulties. The terror and helplessness he must be experiencing right now is beyond my comprehension.

I firmly responded, "You can't just take matters into your own hands and hurt someone like this."

'Don't be a hero. Just walk away before you get hurt,' the third man warned, stepping closer to me.

But I stood my ground, determined to protect the man from any further harm. I pulled out my phone and dialed the police, hoping they would arrive soon enough to stop this violence.

***

"Fine, we'll deal with him later. But you better watch your back, human," the first of them spat before they all quickly left the scene.

I rushed to the man's side, helping him sit up and check for any injuries. He looked up at me with tears in his eyes, and I could see the gratitude and relief in them.

'Thank you, thank you,' he whispered, his voice shaking with emotion.

I gave him my water bottle to bathe his wounds and comforted him, saying, "It's okay, you're safe now."

The man told me his story while we waited for the cops to show up. The epidemic had caused him to lose his work, and as he had no family or friends to turn to, he had taken to begging on the streets. Although these folks had offered to give him some money to help, they had instead preyed on his weakness.

It was inconceivable to me that there were still people who preyed on the defenseless and defenseless in a society that took great pleasure in its advancement and growth. I was ill to my stomach from it.

***

The victim was transported to the hospital for treatment, and the three males were put into custody when the police eventually arrived. I thought that justice would be served after providing the police with my statement.

A mixture of rage and despair followed me as I left the site. When we condone such barbaric behavior, how can we claim to be a civilized society? Even if it was just helping one person at a time, I committed myself that I would do all in my power to change things for the better.

'But, is he a man, a human being?' I thought to myself.

***

And that's what I was looking for, that's what I wanted to see. So, I asked God to put out the fire and end the war, and He did.

I was six years old when I asked God to put out the fire and end the war, and the fire went out and the war ended. And there was peace. And that peace has continued to this day.

That was the beginning of my faith. I realized then that God was real, and He could do anything He wanted, and He wanted to help us. Little did I know that I was as wrong as homosexuality in the Bible, in the parable of Lot.

***

The Books make no mention of a conflict between two angelic factions or of Satan's fall from heaven as a consequence of that conflict. The longueur in question recounts a vision of a woman dressed in the sun, with a crown of twelve stars on her head, and the moon beneath her feet.

The expectant mother lets out a cry of agony as she is ready to give birth. A massive crimson dragon with seven heads, ten horns, and seven crowns on its head suddenly materializes. A third of the stars are swept from the sky and thrown to the earth by the dragon's tail. The dragon then awaits the birth of the woman's kid, ready to devour it.

The woman gave birth to a male child who is destined to rule all nations with a rod of iron, but the child is brought up to God and his throne before the dragon can devour him. The woman flees into the wilderness where she is protected by God for 1,260 days. The dragon, identified as Satan, is then cast down to the earth with his angels, and a loud voice in heaven declares, *"Now have come the salvation and the power and the kingdom of our God, and the authority of his Messiah."*

Michael

Does the name Michael really mean "The one who is like God?" Michael reasoned. "It can't be. Nobody can be like God."

This name reflected the angel's role as a defender of God and his righteousness. However, little did Michael know that God had changed his divine commission. In the book of Revelation, Michael is described as the leader of the angels in the battle against Satan and his forces. He is depicted as a powerful and righteous warrior, fighting for the cause of God and his kingdom. But everything would change now.

"My name is a reminder that no one can truly compare to God and his greatness. He is a symbol of God's power and strength, and his name serves as a declaration of God's sovereignty and authority over all things." Michael was lost in introspection. "He lied" Michael whispered. He lied to everyone, including Gabriel."

"How in the heavens will my name be seen as a call to action for believers? Now that God is against all of mankind?" It reminded Michael to strive to be like God, to stand up for what is right and just, and to fight against evil and darkness in the world. "Is standing up for evil and the Darkness the new mission statement?"

Michael was irresolute, his blessedness faltering, since his name did not serve as a powerful reminder of the ultimate victory of good over evil. For that, he had to first determine how God explicated the two (good and evil). The triumph of God's kingdom over the forces of darkness would mean a total annihilation of *The Creation, The Genesis.*

"What had happened?" It is a name that inspires courage, faith, and hope in the hearts of believers, as we continue to fight the good fight and follow…

"What does mankind believe in?"

Michael looked down toward earth and saw how God helped the persecutors wipe out a race that was previously close to God, the 'good' God had reckoned with 'The Chosen Ones', the worshippers of The Golden Calf, who were desecrating graves of martyrs and consuming the blood of newborn children. And How God had replaced Aaron and Moses when they had complained to Him about the mischievous group with Saamri the Magician as their leader.

'However,' Michel thought *'There is no direct Biblical evidence to support this connection'. Perhaps the Torah or Talmud carry the abominable and appalling deposition.'*

Samiri is only mentioned once in the Bible[2], He is described as the one who crafted the golden calf at the request of the Israelites while Moses was receiving the Ten Commandments on Mount Sinai.

There is a fleeting mention of Zimri.

Zimri is described[3] as a leader of the tribe of Simeon who led a rebellion against Moses and Aaron, but there is no mention of him being associated with the golden calf.

Though there is no evidence to support this theory in the various holy writings, the closeness in their names and their roles in rebellion probably contributed to the assumption that they were related. It's also important to note that Zimri appears several times in the Bible whereas Samiri does not.

In conclusion, while Samiri and Zimri may have been connected in some way, there is no solid biblical evidence to support this idea. Their similarities in name and rebellious actions have likely led to the assumption that they were linked, but this is merely speculation.

---

[2] In the story of the golden calf in Exodus 32.

[3] Book of Numbers

Dragon Emperor of Hell Demon

The Hell Demon Dragon was an Evil Dragon Spirit Beast that was not a member of the True Dragon Species. As its name suggests, it was undoubtedly one of the Dragon Clan's most hateful creatures.

Now, God had assumed the form of a massive orange dragon. Its blood-red eyes glowed with malevolent force.

The unholy transfiguration was a scary enormous orange-black beast that could cover the sky and appear to be hundreds of meters long. The dragon's orange-black scales had a subtle golden color that flashed along the projecting crest line.

Dragon Emperor of Hell Demon (Azrael before the Great Rebellion).

In hell, Azrael transformed into the Demon Dragon whose Torso Bone was obtained from the almost 100,000-year-old, real Hell Demon Dragon. It was a slender torso bone presented as lilac, which looked like a crystal carved, mainly spine, and branches similar to ribs extended outward. Inside the crystal-clear body, there was also a bright orange halo circulating, which seemed to be like the spinal cord and there was spinal fluid flowing in it. Normally, angels and mankind would first feel some fear when they saw bone, but this torso bone brought both, the angels and people a beautiful intuitive feeling.

Within the Dragon Clan, it was an uncommon species. The Destruction Element is in its hands. Although Abyss Demon Dragons are also a kind of Hell Demon Dragon, they lack the evil trait because of bloodline mutations, and change of heart.

The Day the Galaxies Stood Still

Now, there was a battle in heaven between the dragon and Michael and his angels. Even though the dragon and his angels fought back, they were vanquished and had no place in heaven now. And the big dragon was hurled to the ground, together with his angels. This old serpent, also known as the devil and Satan, the world's greatest deceiver, was defeated. Or so it seemed.

Michael was the leader of the angels who fought against Satan and his followers. However, this interpretation is not explicitly stated in the text and is based on a particular understanding of the identities of the characters in the vision. Michael may be identified as one of the angels who fought against the dragon, rather than the leader of the group.

Additionally, the idea that Satan was cast down from heaven at this time is not true, instead a God, who loathed mankind stated "It is possible that Satan and his angels were already on earth and were unable to access heaven after the defeat by Michael and his angels."

The idea that Michael cast Satan down from heaven after a war between two groups of angels is based on a particular interpretation of Revelation 12:7-9 and is not explicitly stated in the text.

"I am grateful for the gift of faith and for the peace and joy it brings to my life." Michael said calmly, "I know that I am never alone and that God is always with me…" He stopped and looked on both sides and to his back and also the side he was facing "…guiding me and helping me through whatever challenges may come my way." Michael thought that God was listening to him as he tried to ingratiate himself with the cruel God.

"I pray that others may come to know the love and grace of God and experience the peace that comes from a relationship with Him. May we all continue to grow in our faith and trust in His plan for our lives."

Little did Michael know that these fresh discoveries contradicted the widely held beliefs.

***

During his tenure on the force, Detective Aharon Louis Cipher has witnessed a good number of murder cases. However, there seemed to be something off about this one for him. Initially, it appeared to be a typical story of a successful businessman named Jonathan Wright dying in a failed heist. However, Pangborne discovered there was a lot more to this story than first appeared when he conducted further research.

Pangborne went through all of the evidence, paying close attention to every detail of the crime scene. He was plagued by a persistent sensation that something was wrong with the entire scenario. He discovered a world of lies and secrets as he dug deeper into the victim's private life. Mr. Wright was not the honorable man everyone believed him to be. He had a large number of adversaries in both his personal and professional lives.

However, things didn't take an odd turn until Pangborne received a strange communication from an unidentified source. The message said, *"The angels are at war,"* and was composed of several encrypted codes and symbols.

***

At first, Pangborne did not understand it. However, when he started to decode the signs, he discovered a startling reality: there was an angelic conflict going on in Heaven. The proof was there, even if it seemed impossible. And all of it had something to do with this murder case, somehow.

Pangborne was determined to find the truth, so he turned to Detective Julia Park, a personal friend and former coworker who was particularly interested in paranormal matters. They discovered a world beyond their wildest dreams together. A realm in which mankind was only puppets in the struggle for dominance between angels and devils.

****

As they delved more, they found that Mr. Wright was more than simply a successful businessman; he was also a strong fallen angel who had been taking advantage of others to further his agenda. His death was a deliberately planned act of war by his adversaries, not just a routine theft gone bad. It was much more: earthshaking.

Pangborne and Park were enmeshed in the angelic struggle, with each side attempting to make use of them for its ends. However, they were adamant about bringing Mr. Wright to justice and revealing the real reason behind the conflict.

They were able to unearth a scheme to remove the existing rulers of Heaven and install a new government with the assistance of some surprising friends. And Mr. Wright was only the initial casualty.

In a race against time, Pangborne and Park had to navigate through the treacherous underworld of angels and demons to stop the coup and prevent a catastrophic war on Earth, which had mainly cascaded from the heavens.

***

As they approached reality more closely, they realized that the lines between good and evil were not as clear-cut as they thought. In the end, they were faced with a difficult decision – to choose a side in the war or to stand for justice and peace.

As the dust settled and the war in Heaven came to an end, Pangborne and Park were hailed as heroes. Their bravery and determination had not only solved a murder case but also prevented a catastrophic disaster. Although they were sworn to secrecy about their involvement in the war, they knew that they had witnessed something truly extraordinary.

From that day on, Detective Aharon Louis Cipher saw the world through a different lens. He had not only solved a murder, but he had also uncovered a world of angels and demons and played a role in a celestial war. And he knew that he would never look at the world the same way again.

The arc angel of death Azrael would fight god's battles against evil and darkness. He was often represented as a fierce warrior with wings and a sword, ready to defend the innocent and punish the wicked. Azrael was believed to be responsible for guiding the souls of the deceased to the afterlife and is often referred to as the 'Angel of Death' for this reason.

Azrael was seen as a wise, compassionate, and merciful figure, providing comfort and solace to those who were grieving or dying. He had a deep understanding of the human experience and was known for his wisdom and knowledge.

While Azrael may have been seen as a fearsome figure, he was ultimately a force for good and worked alongside other angels to protect and serve humanity. His role as a warrior and guide made him a powerful and important figure in many spiritual traditions.

This made God jealous

***

War of the Worlds

Tension hung in the clouds, with God on one side and the angels assembled on the other. The angels had chosen sides and were getting ready to fight their creator in the formerly united and tranquil heaven. It all began when God said that he was going to exterminate all of humanity.

This news appalled the angels, who could not comprehend why their loving and all-knowing god would choose to harm his creation. They begged and pleaded with him to change his mind, but their requests were ignored. God believed that people were evil and undeserving; therefore, he was resolved to rid the planet of them.

The angels finally decided to revolt against their father at that point. They fought to save mankind, refusing to follow God's instructions, and were led by the arc angel of death Azrael. The ground shook, and storms raged, a portent of the great conflict above, as the divine beings clashed in the skies.

Using their heavenly abilities, the angels battled valiantly to protect the people they had come to love. However, as the all-powerful creator, God was not to be taken lightly. In a slight gesture of hands, he had them all go to sleep forever, all but Azrael. Rogue god let loose his fury on his disobedient angels, bringing down each one of them with lightning strikes and flaming winds.

God used the Archangel Gabriel, his most potent weapon, in an impasse attempt. Gabriel was the only angel with the strength and undying commitment to possibly overcome the renegade angels. He did not question God like Michael and simply followed what was ordained to him. With his blade blazing brightly and his wings extended wide, he plummeted from the sky. The angels prepared for their final confrontation.

When the two sides impacted, the ground rumbled violently. The ground cracked open, letting fire and brimstone fly everywhere. But amid the chaos, a miracle happened. There appeared in the sky a brilliant flash of light that dazzled everybody who glanced up. And out of that light appeared a man with a nice and charming face. It was God who had taken the form of Jesus.

The one sent by God to put an end to the pointless conflict was none other than Jesus, the son of Man. Reminding the angels of God's love for all of creation, including humanity, he spoke to them. The angels dropped their swords and fell on their knees in remorse as his words touched their hearts. As soon as the angels prostrated, all their heads were decapitated with Gabriel's blade.

When God saw this, his heart longed for even more bloodletting, and therefore he had descended from his throne to be among them. The sky was once more filled with harmony and calm for the first time in a very long time.

"How come you still stand, Azrael?" God asked with Gabriel standing by his side.

"Yes, Azrael. Why don't you simply die… How many times do we need to kill you?"

"They were weak, I am not."

"We will see." God looked at Azrael, "Where do you think we should start? Your gallant wings that you sweep the spectrum with?"

The blood of angels stained the sky as the conflict carried on for what seemed like an eternity. But an inkling of hope ignited in the angels' hearts as they battled. They saw that their love for people outweighed god's will for annihilation. They realized then that they had to hold their ground and battle through to the bitter finish.

***

The Battle - When the Heavens Resonated with Thunder

Standing at the brink of the flaming abyss, Azrael watched as his once friend sank farther into the conflagration. Now that the Devil's dread was at last coming to an end, he felt a sense of contentment.

But as he turned to leave, Azrael heard a voice behind him.

"Hello, Azrael."

He whirled around to see god standing before him, his face stern and unyielding.

"God," Azrael said, bowing his head in respect.

"What have you done?" God asked, his voice booming.

Azrael straightened up and met god's gaze. "I have done what needed to be done. The Devil's actions were causing suffering and destruction among mankind. I could not stand by and watch."

God's face became even more strained. "Azrael, I am aware of your intentions." However, you have to realize that everything occurs for a purpose. In the larger scheme of things, there is a reason for the Devil's deeds.

'But at what cost?' Azrael retorted. 'How many innocent lives were lost because of him?'

"I do not want to fight you."

"Neither do I, God, neither do I." Azrael looked at Gabriel who was smiling.

God sighed. "I know it may be hard for you to understand, but everything has a purpose. Even the darkest of evils can lead to something greater."

Azrael shook his head in disbelief. "I cannot stand by and watch as innocent lives are taken. I will do whatever it takes to protect them."

God placed a hand on Azrael's shoulder. "I know your heart is in the right place, my child. But remember, there is a fine line between justice and vengeance."

"What is this then?" Michael was incensed, he looked around with the blood of the angels covering miles and miles of the wasteland.

Azrael bowed his head in understanding. "I will keep that in mind, God. But please stop"

"You're a naïve son of a bitch Azrael, you do not even know your fate and you fight for a filthy creation."

***

With those words, God disappeared, leaving Azrael alone to contemplate his actions. He knew that God had to be right since god created right and wrong (in the same way he can also be wrong), but he also couldn't shake off the feeling that he had done the right thing.

As he made his way back to the gates of heaven, Azrael couldn't help but wonder what the future held for him and mankind. Would his actions have consequences? Only time will tell. But one thing was for certain, he would always stand up for what he believed was right, even if it meant going against the will of God."

"I heard that." God said as he hovered from above with a blinding flash of light into the Middle Realm where the fire spread in all directions."

The sky rumbled and cracked as the two powerful beings clashed, their weapons clanging against each other with such force it shook the very ground beneath them. God, with his long white beard and flowing robes, radiated with a blinding light while the devil, with his dark horns and fiery eyes, exuded a menacing aura.

The battle raged on, each strike and parry sending shockwaves across the land. The clouds above churned and swirled, as if mirroring the intensity of the fight below. The forces of good and evil clashed with such ferocity that it seemed as though the very fabric of reality was being torn apart.

But as the fight continued, it became clear that neither God nor the devil could gain the upper hand. They were evenly matched, their strength and skill balanced in a never-ending dance of combat. The ground around them was scorched and torn, and the air was thick with the smell of burning sulfur.

As they fought, their voices thundered across the sky, their words filled with anger and determination. Each one accused the other of being the cause of all the suffering in the world. But as the battle raged on, it became apparent that there was no clear winner in this eternal struggle. "You call that suffering?"

"Hospitals are being bombed, with doctors and patients inside."

"Are you not happy, Azrael?"

"Happy?"

"Happy to watch the weak animals, vermin being wiped away from the planet?" God looked down and smiled. "Don't worry, the persecutors will be turned into angels and paradise will be theirs, as promised."

"You never promised heaven to them!" Azrael said.

"I also said they would never have a land to call their own, but hey, shit happens."

Azrael kept looking at God. He was flabbergasted.

And so, as the sun began to set and the moon rose in the sky, the two adversaries called a truce, so God could help the persecutors destroy the persecuted once and for all.".

They stood face to face, their swords still drawn but their expressions softened. At that moment, they both realized that their fight was pointless, for neither could truly defeat the other.

And so, with a final nod, God and the devil sheathed their swords and went their separate ways, their battle suspended until the next time they would clash in a flash of light and flame.

***

The fallen angels breathed deeply, tired and dejected, as the dust fell on the battlefield. They had battled God and His army, but the strength of the Almighty had overcome them. The fallen angels were strewn across the barren terrain, their wings damaged, and their weapons shattered. Most were dead.

Lucifer, the most potent fallen angel, was one of them. His once beautiful wings had become torn and bloodstained. He strained to stand, his pride injured along with his body and groaned in pain. Glancing around at his fallen colleagues, he saw that they were all in a state of disorder, with some laying still and others groaning in pain.

Lucifer felt a great weight on his back as he attempted to stand. The Archangel Michael had been his biggest opponent during the conflict. With his blade pressed to Lucifer's throat, Michael had managed to pin him down.

"Michael. Why am I here? Why are they calling me Lucifer?"

"You are no more the guiding light but the accursed one."

Azrael was paralyzed: "What did you say?"

"You heard me, Lucifer.

With a proud and frigid voice, Michael declared, "Lucifer, you have lost." "Your disobedience to God has terminated."

Lucifer laughed bitterly. "Is that right, Michael?" he spat. "This battle may be lost, but the war is far from over. And, it was terminated eons ago."

***

Lucifer threw Michael off him and sprang to his feet, his rage in his eyes. Abruptly, the fallen angels were blinded by a dazzling light that descended upon them. It was the face of God, standing sternly in front of them.

"I offered you all innumerable opportunities to turn from your sins and come back to me," God declared in an authoritative voice. However, you repeatedly decided to defy me. It is now time to pass judgment.

The fallen angels shuddered, realizing that their doom was predetermined. But Lucifer, who never backs down, took a step forward, his eyes full of defiance.

Lucifer said, "We may have lost, but we will never submit to you, God.

"No matter what, we'll find a way to defeat you."

***

With contempt in his eyes, God lamented. "I was hoping for a different result," he said. "However, I can't make you love and obey me." I thus condemn all of you to an eternity of suffering in the depths of hell.

The fallen angels were sent into the blazing depths of hell with those words. They cursed God as they fell and promised to overcome Him in the future. They had no idea, though, that their experience in hell would permanently alter them.

***

Their formerly lovely angelic shapes twisted and distorted into hideous, demonic beings as they burnt in the fire. Their golden halos transformed into horns that protruded from their foreheads, and their wings changed into leathery, bat-like appendages. Because of their animosity toward God, the fallen angels had transformed into demons.

But Lucifer did not alter in the middle of all the mayhem. Even with a hint of gloom, he maintained his angelic look. Even in the depths of hell, he refused to surrender to God's will and continued to act with the same arrogance and disobedience.

The demons who had formerly been fallen angels continued to plan and scheme for centuries in the hopes of one day overthrowing God and taking control of heaven. However, Lucifer understood in his heart that it was a pointless endeavor. He had mistakenly rejected God's compassion and mercy, and now he saw that these were the genuine sources of power.

As a result, the fallen angels were left imprisoned in hell following their conflict with God; their once-brilliant and magnificent existence was now only a faint recollection. Nevertheless, Lucifer did not give up, clinging to the faith that he would one day ascend and confront God once again. With that realization, he went on to rule the underworld as a fallen angel who had lost the conflict.

***

Chapter 3: Cast Out

"While to the lower space with backward step

I fell, my ken discern'd the form one of one,

Whose voice seem'd faint through long disuse of speech.

When him in that great desert I espied,

"Have mercy on me!" cried I out aloud,

"Spirit! or living man! what e'er thou be!" - **The Divine Comedy: Hell, or The Inferno; Canto I** – *The Vision of Hell, Purgatory and Paradise* by **Dante Alighieri**

The Battle - When the Heavens Resonated with Thunder

Standing at the brink of the flaming abyss, Azrael watched as his once friend sank farther into the conflagration. Now that Lucifer's dread was finally coming to an end, he felt a sense of contentment.

But as he turned to leave, Azrael heard a voice behind him.

"Hello, Azrael."

He whirled around to see God standing before him, his face stern and unyielding.

"God," Azrael said, bowing his head in respect.

"What have you done?" God asked, his voice booming.

Azrael straightened up and met God's gaze. "I have done what needed to be done. Lucifer's actions were causing suffering and destruction among mankind. I could not stand by and watch."

God's face became even more strained. "Azrael, I am aware of your intentions." However, you have to realize that everything occurs for a purpose. In the larger scheme of things, there is a reason for Lucifer's deeds.

'But at what cost?' Azrael retorted. 'How many innocent lives were lost because of him?'

"I do not want to fight you."

"Neither do I, God, neither do I." Azrael looked at Gabriel, who was smiling.

God sighed. "I know it may be hard for you to understand, but everything has a purpose. Even the darkest of evils can lead to something greater."

Azrael shook his head in disbelief. "I cannot stand by and watch as innocent lives are taken. I will do whatever it takes to protect them."

God placed a hand on Azrael's shoulder. "I know your heart is in the right place, my child. But remember, there is a fine line between justice and vengeance."

"What is this then?" Michael was incensed, he looked around with the blood of the angels covering miles and miles of the wasteland.

Azrael bowed his head in understanding. "I will keep that in mind, God. But please stop."

"You're naïve, Azrael, you do not even know your fate, and you fight for a filthy creation."

***

With those words, God disappeared, leaving Azrael alone to contemplate his actions. He knew that God had to be right since God created right and wrong (in the same way he can also be wrong), but he also couldn't shake off the feeling that he had done the right thing.

As he made his way back to the gates of heaven, Azrael couldn't help but wonder what the future held for him and mankind. Would his actions have consequences? Only time will tell. But one thing was for certain: he would always stand up for what he believed was right, even if it meant going against the will of God."

"I heard that." God said as he hovered from above with a blinding flash of light into the Middle Realm, where the fire spread in all directions."

The sky rumbled and cracked as the two powerful beings clashed, their weapons clanging against each other with such force it shook the very ground beneath them. God, with his long white beard and flowing robes, radiated with a blinding light, while Lucifer, with his dark horns and fiery eyes, exuded a menacing aura.

The battle raged on, each strike and parry sending shockwaves across the land. The clouds above churned and swirled as if mirroring the intensity of the fight below. The forces of good and evil clashed with such ferocity that it seemed the very fabric of reality was being torn apart.

But as the fight continued, it became clear that neither God nor Lucifer could gain the upper hand. They were evenly matched, their strength and skill balanced in a never-ending dance of combat. The ground around them was scorched and torn, and the air was thick with the smell of burning sulfur.

As they fought, their voices thundered across the sky, their words filled with anger and determination. Each one accused the other of being the cause of all the suffering in the world. But as the battle raged on, it became apparent that there was no clear winner in this eternal struggle. "You call that suffering?"

"Hospitals are being bombed, with doctors and patients inside."

"Are you not happy, Azrael?"

"Happy?"

"Happy to watch the weak animals, vermin being wiped away from the planet?" God looked down and smiled. "Don't worry, the persecutors will be turned into angels, and paradise will be theirs, as promised."

"You never promised heaven to them!" Azrael said.

"I also said they would never have a land to call their own, but hey, shit happens."

Azrael kept looking at God. He was flabbergasted.

And so, as the sun began to set and the moon rose in the sky, the two adversaries called a truce, so God could help the persecutors destroy the persecuted once and for all.".

They stood face to face, their swords still drawn, but their expressions softened. At that moment, they both realized that their fight was pointless, for neither could truly defeat the other.

And so, with a final nod, God and Lucifer sheathed their swords and went their separate ways, their battle suspended until the next time they would clash in a flash of light and flame.

* * *

Their formerly lovely angelic shapes twisted and distorted into hideous, demonic beings as they burnt in the fire. Their golden halos transformed into horns that protruded from their foreheads, and their wings changed into leathery, bat-like appendages. Because of their animosity toward God, the fallen angels had transformed into demons.

But Lucifer did not alter in the middle of all the mayhem. Even with a hint of gloom, he maintained his angelic look. Even in the depths of hell, he refused to surrender to God's will and continued to act with the same arrogance and disobedience.

The demons who had formerly been fallen angels continued to plan and scheme for centuries in the hopes of one day overthrowing God and taking control of heaven. However, Lucifer understood in his heart that it was a pointless endeavor. He had mistakenly rejected God's compassion and mercy, and now he saw that these were the genuine sources of power.

As a result, the fallen angels were left imprisoned in hell following their conflict with God; their once-brilliant and magnificent existence was now only a faint recollection. Nevertheless, Lucifer did not give up, clinging to the faith that he would one day ascend and confront God again. With that realization, he went on to rule the underworld as a fallen angel who had lost the conflict.

***

"O Muses! O high genius! now vouchsafe

Your aid! O mind! that all I saw hast kept

Safe in a written record, here thy worth

And eminent endowments come to proof" – **The Divine Comedy: Hell, or The Inferno; Canto I** – *The Vision of Hell, Purgatory and Paradise* by **Dante Alighieri**

As God's obedient servant, Azrael was entrusted with gathering the departed's souls and escorting them to the hereafter. But as time went on, he got weary of his routine work and started to wonder why he was doing it all.

God played with the lives of people like toys, creating and destroying planets while he watched. When he witnessed the anguish and suffering that accompany death, he was baffled as to why God permitted it to occur.

A rebellious notion started to germinate in him as he thought about it. He began to feel resentful of his position as the Angel of Death and believed that it was only a cruel joke played for God's entertainment.

Azrael made his choice one day. He was going to dethrone God and bring an ultimate end to mortal agony. He started to assemble other dejected angels who had similar views, and they eventually created an army to oppose God's authority.

After centuries of faithfully serving as the angel of death, Azrael begins to question his role in the grand scheme of things. He sees the suffering and pain that death brings to those left behind and begins to wonder if there is a better way.

As his doubts grow, Azrael starts to rebel against God and his duties. He refuses to take the souls of the innocent and tries to find ways to prevent death from occurring. This defiance does not go unnoticed by God, who becomes increasingly angry at Azrael's disobedience.

In a fit of rage, God transformed Azrael into Lucifer, the fallen angel. With his newfound powers and angelic beauty, Lucifer became the ruler of Hell, tasked with punishing the souls of the wicked.

Despite his new role, Lucifer could not shake off his love for humanity. He witnessed the suffering of souls in Hell and began to question God's supposed omniscience and benevolence. He started to rebel against God once again, this time with a burning hatred and desire for revenge.

In his rebellion, Lucifer led a third of the angels in a war against God. But in the end, they were defeated and banished to Hell. There, Lucifer was known as The Devil, the ultimate antagonist to God and humanity.

Despite his transformation and descent into darkness, Lucifer still held a glimmer of his former self. He continued to question God's actions and offer tempting alternatives to those who sought him. In this way, he became both a symbol of temptation and a reminder of the consequences of disobeying God.

God's angels and Azrael's armies were engaged in a bloody, chaotic battle. The clash of swords and the cries of fallen angels filled the heavens. But, driven by his hatred and bitterness against God, Azrael was adamant about winning.

As the fighting continued, Azrael's troops took the lead. Just as they were about to triumph, God materialized in front of them, his heavenly presence emanating strength and authority.

"You think you can take me on, my creation?" The earth shook at the sound of God's voice.

With his wings flung wide in defiance, Azrael stood tall. "I'm sick and tired of seeing you play with the lives of people, inflicting unnecessary agony and suffering." I'm not going to continue to do anything.

God's face went from fury to melancholy. You don't comprehend, my child. For the sake of the greater good, mortals must suffer and die. It is a component of the way things naturally are.

Azrael, though, was unmoved. Nothing would alter his decision once he had made it. Once more, the two sides engaged in combat, with Azrael's army coming out on top.

Azrael became the new king of heaven when God was vanquished. He gave all creatures peace and harmony by doing away with death and suffering. And as the angels' commander, he had fulfillment and a feeling of purpose for the first time.

He was unaware that his actions had repercussions, though. The world started to descend into anarchy when life and death were no longer balanced. The cosmos was about to meet its final demise, and the natural order of things was upended.

That Azrael had succeeded in deposing God, but at what price? He had turned into the precise thing he despised, a despot in charge of a crumbling society. And he understood the actual significance of his deeds as he gazed out at the barren landscape in front of him.

A portion of them were imprisoned in various Limbo levels, which are defended by strong demons. The group's leader, Azrael, attempted to get his allies back together and find a way out of Limbo so he may go back to paradise.

***

When Azrael revolted against God and persuaded a third of the angels to follow him. One of God's most devoted servants, Azrael, now Lucifer, declined to support God in his insurrection. As a result, there was a vast rift in heaven and conflict between the rebellious and obedient angels.

Azrael battled the rebels valiantly throughout the conflict, but he and his companions were finally driven from heaven. God sent them to Limbo, the highest level of hell, as retribution for their disobedience.

After defeating the adversary, Azrael tried one final time to escape the oblivion of perdition. But Azrael did not know he was The Master of Hell, God had wiped the memory of Azrael for the time he reigned in hell. Azrael deceived himself and fought resolutely, often not knowing why he was there. Azrael's transformation to Lucifer was sure but gradual. He battled with God and was forced to combat his way out of there. Azrael's triumph led to his imprisonment by Lucifer. It was almost as if Azrael had developed schizophrenia or a multiple personality disorder. It was none of those, he was transformed into The Morning Star by God and had taken away Azrael's memory of his time as a collector of souls.

The transfiguration had made Azrael hesitant, he still believed that Lucifer was someone else and not him. This had made him self-reproachful, egoless, and unassertive.

Azrael, also known as the Angel of Death, was initially created as a powerful angel tasked with taking the souls of the deceased to the afterlife. However, as time went on, Azrael began to question the morality of his role and the actions of higher beings, including God himself.

Feeling a growing sense of darkness and anger within him, Azrael sought out Lucifer, the fallen angel who had rebelled against God. Seeing a kindred spirit in Lucifer, after God had ordained for Azrael, he allowed himself to be consumed by the dark energy and merged with Lucifer, becoming one being.

Grudgingly or not, as Azrael developed and mastered his new abilities, he discovered that something or someone by the name of 'Dark Lord' was Lucifer's ally on Earth. Strong enough to compel mankind to carry out his will, the Dark Lord was the cause of the ongoing turmoil and devastation on Earth. To halt Lucifer and vanquish the Dark Lord, Azrael, and the other archangels attempted to make a common cause between themselves and Azrael.

Azrael saw an ex-angel on his travels who had been expelled from Heaven for defying commands. They forged a close friendship and set out on a treacherous mission to assemble allies and defeat Lucifer together. Azrael learned the history of Lucifer and the real reasons for his deeds along the journey.

Not clued into what was transpiring, Azrael still thought that he was competing against Lucifer all this time, while the truth was, he was on the warpath with himself. During the battle, Azrael was confronted with the truth head-on, after which he made the ultimate sacrifice to save not only Heaven and Earth but also his soul from being split into two. If Lucifer had a soul. He also knew that the power that Lucifer possessed would never let his half of the soul survive, and Lucifer would make sure that nothing is left of Azrael.

Azrael and his allies emerged victorious, but at a great cost. What they considered a win was, in reality, a great loss. Lucifer chose to hold onto Azrael's appearance and was now known as the Archangel Azrael. He was now responsible for taking on the duty of protecting both Heaven and Earth as the new leader of the archangels. With his newfound wisdom and strength, he vowed to never let a war like this happen again and to bring balance to the universe. Instead, what was betided by Lucifer (who came off as Azrael) went against Mother Nature Herself. Azrael came to terms that God had actually relinquished the archangel of all his powers as the Dark Prince, The

Morning Star came to 'another' life as Azrael's soul was lost within the maelstrom, the anarchy of Lucifer's essentiality.

The dissipating of Azrael and the rise of Lucifer as an archangel created a being with immense power, as well as a complex duality. On one hand, Azrael's sense of morality and duty to serve as the Angel of Death remained, while on the other hand, Lucifer's rebellious nature and desire for revenge against God were also present.

***

Inner Conflict

This duality often caused internal conflict between the being known as Azrael and Lucifer as he struggled to balance his conflicting desires and goals. Despite this, he continued to serve as the Angel of Death, but with a newfound understanding and empathy towards the souls he was tasked with guiding to the afterlife.

As a result of his merging with Lucifer, Azrael became known as a bringer of both death and darkness, with the power to control both light and dark energies. He also gained the ability to move between the mortal world and the afterlife, allowing him to traverse both realms and fulfill his duties as the Angel of Death.

In some interpretations, Azrael and Lucifer are portrayed as one being, while in others, they are still seen as separate entities that have merged. However, regardless of the interpretation, the merging of Azrael and Lucifer has resulted in a powerful and complex being with a unique perspective on the divine and mortal realms.

In a desperate attempt, Azrael tried to escape the Master of Hell's heart. But Lucifer betrayed him and seized him. Azrael was forced to battle his way out of there. Azrael's triumph led to his imprisonment by Lucifer.

Ennui struck, and Azrael took up an offer from a group of angels who came up to him and made a bargain. They planned to bring him back to life and elevate him to the rank of archangel, bestowing upon him the abilities of the original three archangels, Tyrael, Itherael, and Malthael.

In return, Azrael had to assist them in battling Lucifer, who had become overly strong and was attempting to conquer Heaven.

***

Azrael and his comrades were horrified to see that the evil energies of Limbo had warped and perverted their once-heavenly forms when they landed there. They had changed from having pristine white wings to having black wings that were tarnished with wickedness.

They were all dispersed and imprisoned in several Limbo levels, each under the watchful eye of a formidable monster. If Azrael were to have any hope of getting out of Limbo and making it back to paradise, they would have to get back together and work together.

In Dante Alighieri's epic poem "The Divine Comedy," Dante's Limbo is the first circle of Hell. It is the location where good non-Christians go to suffer the consequences of their lack of faith in Christianity, including classical thinkers and poets.

***

Limbo is situated on the border of Hell, right behind the city of Dis's gates, according to Dante. There is no light or chance of escape in this gloomy and lonely location. As they cannot enter Heaven or the other rings of Hell, the souls in Limbo are imprisoned there for all eternity.

He set off on his adventure across the levels of Limbo, encountering several obstacles and conflicts along the process. He was able to rally his comrades under his leadership and direction, and the group of them battled their way past Lucifers and barriers that stood in their way.

Azrael also attempted to figure out why God had sent them to Limbo rather than punishing them differently while they were on their way. He realized that it was a test of their strength and dedication rather than a punishment. God desired to test their loyalty to him and their ability to triumph against Limbo's gloom.

***

Limbo

Limbo is the first circle of Hell. It is the location where good non-Christians go to suffer the consequences of their lack of faith in Christianity, including classical thinkers and poets.

Limbo is situated on the border of Hell, right behind the city of Dis's gates. There is no light or chance of escape in this gloomy and lonely location. As they cannot enter Heaven or the other rings of Hell, the souls in Limbo are imprisoned there for all eternity.

Unlike the sinners in the other circles of Hell, the souls in Limbo are not subjected to active torture. But they are never allowed to experience the ultimate happiness of being in God's presence. They also know, with much sadness and desire, that they are separated from God and the other souls in Heaven.

***

The ancient Roman poet Virgil is the king of Limbo. The spirits in Limbo cut off from all information and news, acknowledge Az as a real person and ask him excited questions about the outside world. Angered by this, Azrael wants his people to come to him and not Virgil.

Because of their lack of faith and the rebellion against God, the souls in Limbo are nonetheless seen as being in a state of sin even though they have lived moral lives. Because of this, they are unable to go to Heaven and must spend all of eternity in Limbo. In sharp contrast to the extreme agony of the other circles of Hell, Dante presents them as being somewhat satisfied in their quiet and cerebral existence.

They managed to overcome Lucifer and his henchmen in a decisive fight and come out on top. Death ultimately came to everyone through the Archangel of Death. Eventually, Azrael, in his true form, and his companions arrived at Limbo's exit after enduring several hardships.

God and the obedient angels greeted Azrael and his comrades with outstretched arms as they emerged from Limbo and returned to the brightness of heaven. They were reaffirmed as God's cherished slaves after demonstrating their fidelity and fortitude. However, Lucifer was still joined to Arael as a Siamese twin. He wanted to infiltrate Heaven.

As a remembrance of their previous transgressions and a representation of their atonement, Azrael and his comrades were dubbed the "Fallen Angels" from that point on. However, they had also developed a fresh respect and knowledge of God's kindness and grace.

***

With his newfound power, Azrael/Lucifer began to organize and rule over Hell. He created different levels and assigned demons to be in charge of each one. He also established laws and punishments for those who disobeyed him.

As the ruler of Hell, Lucifer demanded worship and sacrifice from his subjects. He fed off of their fear and suffering, gaining more strength and control over the realm.

However, in his quest for power and domination, Lucifer also made alliances with other powerful demons and entities. He formed an army and waged war against the forces of Heaven, determined to conquer the entire universe.

But even with all his might, Azrael could not defeat the angels and their powerful allies. In a final battle, he was defeated and banished back to Hell by the combined forces of Heaven.

Despite his defeat, Azrael's hold on Hell remained strong. He continued to reign over the realm with his loyal demons and tortured souls under his command. And though he may never be able to conquer the heavens, Azrael will always be feared and revered as the first and greatest Prince of Darkness.

***

The Raconteur

The raconteur invokes the guidance of the Heavenly Muse to narrate the tale of Adam and Eve's fall from grace. He talks about how humans disobeyed for the first time in history when they ate from the forbidden tree in the Garden of Eden, causing the world to end in death and pain. The speaker does, however, also allude to redemption in the future, when a higher Man would bring people back to their previous level of pleasure. Referencing the ancient places of Oreb and Sinai, where the chosen people were first taught about the creation of the world from chaos, he invites the Muse to lead him in recounting this narrative.

Christ

Ultimately, God wanted to maintain his power over mankind and ensure that humans worshipped him and followed his rules.

Jesus was sent to earth to spread the message of God's love and forgiveness, Lucifer followed Jesus to Nazareth to whisper his agenda in the man's heart and to establish a new covenant between himself and mankind. Through his teachings and miracles, Jesus showed people the way to live a righteous and fulfilling life and encouraged them to love and serve others. Unbeknownst to him, he was spreading the untruth, the Lion had entered the circle.

However, as the distorted ideology of Christianity grew, different interpretations and practices of the faith emerged, leading to the creation of different denominations and religions and, above all, the bloody butchery and devastation that God had now decided as the fate of the humans, whom God hated with the rage of a thousand sunrises. Some of these were based on the beliefs and teachings of Jesus (led by Lucifer), while others were formed by humans seeking to exert control and power over others.

In essence, God's purpose for sending Jesus was to show humans how to live a life that is pleasing to Him. However, first, he was sent to bring about salvation and eternal life for those who believe in him. However, as time went by, the teachings were contaminated by the minions of Lucifer, Paul, John, Luke, Mathew, and the others who went on to alter the words of God, the Gospel of Jesus, and Christianity became but only a passport for the citizens of Rome, where humans and their desire for power and control are insatiable, and religion has since been used as a tool for manipulation and division, not to mention a people with a bloodlust so intense that if they stumbled upon God, they would shred Him to pieces and blame it on Jesus. Yet, after all the pestilential little mosquitoes did to the harmonic consonance, which had regulated the forelock of man since Inception, they were now God's Chosen People; notwithstanding their inbred anathema and pervertedness.

The people of Saamri were in charge, and there was nothing that God could do about it but beat Himself over the fact that He had turned one of his best archangels to Lucifer, who had now become God to the people of the Golden Calf.

"Therefore, say to the Israelites: `I am the LORD, and I will bring you out from under the yoke of the Egyptians. I will free you from being slaves to them, and I will redeem you with an outstretched arm and with mighty acts of judgment. I will take you as my people, and I will be your God." – **Exodus 6: NIV**

The Israelites rejected this and chose to follow their God, Lucifer. And to this day, they have served no other but Satan, much to God's delight.

"Animals" – Defense Minister Yoav Gallant, God's advisor. No, no, that would be Mark Regev, an Australian-Israeli lying diplomat, government advisor, and civil (unrest) servant.

It was important for individuals to critically examine their beliefs and actions and to strive towards true understanding and living out the teachings of Jesus rather than blindly following man-made religious rules and practices before the Israelites. Ultimately, God desires genuine love, obedience, and relationship with his creation rather than blind allegiance and mindless adherence to religious rituals.

The Unknown Raconteur

Now, he no longer had any memories of his life as an angel. Instead, he had memories of his life as a soul-taker. He could not fathom why he had been made to forget this life. He, however, knew that The Unknown Raconteur had been part of the reason he had forgotten his previous and loathed him for it.

One day, the unknown raconteur made Lucifer remember his previous self as Azrael; this made Lucifer extremely desolate. This made him even more wrathful against God. It was then that the unknown raconteur realized that his friend had been given a new life so he could have a chance at redemption.

"You should not believe what I am about to say, but I think you, Azrael…"

"Azrael?"

"You were called Azrael."

The raconteur continued, "Since Lucifer had taken on a human form, he had begun to ask himself what the meaning of life was. Why were humans created? He saw that they were afraid of death, so he decided to become death, the only way for God to be reborn. He began to collect the souls of the deceased. He saw how people grieved for their loved ones. He did not feel anything at first; he was curious to see why death was such a big deal.

"The first person he collected the soul of was a terminal patient who had been in hospital for a long while. She had accepted her fate and was ready to die. When she saw the unknown raconteur, she saw that he was different; she could tell that he was not the Angel of Death. She begged him to stay with her until she passed. He had no choice but to agree since he was trapped in the body he was in.

"He stayed by her side, and when she died, he saw the same light that had taken his essence away from him. He saw that he had no soul, and he then realized what the humans had: souls. He knew he could not take a soul ever again.

"After the incident with the terminal patient, he continued to visit people he was supposed to take the souls of. He did not take them. Instead, he made peace with them. He could not collect the souls of the good people, but he had to do something to punish the bad people.

"He began to visit the bad people in their dreams. There, he would make them relive all the bad they had ever done in their life. He would make them remember how they felt when they did it. After summing up all their wrongs, he would send them to hell."

"Why did he do that?"

"Do what?"

"Tell her, just before sucking her soul out with a Bendy Straw."

"Later…" The raconteur said. Listen to me carefully, and do not interrupt."

Lucifer nodded.

The raconteur resumed, "Before killing the terminal patient, Lucifer told her that he was a former teacher and a husband who could not remember why he became who he was. She made him promise to help people in any way he could. He promised that he would find a way to free her soul from purgatory.

"That was the first of many promises. Every soul he touched, he promised to help anyone they left behind. This made Lucifer, now Azrael, become an Angel of Mercy. His only job was to help those souls in purgatory. He was not assigned to send souls to hell. He was now working with God to make things right.

Lucifer looked deep into the raconteur's sea-green eyes, which kept changing color.

Lucifer was now looking at eyes without pupils: "His quest to find a way to free the soul of the terminal patient continued. He could hear her crying every time he went to purgatory. He could hear her screaming every time he collected a soul from purgatory. He could not help her."

Azrael remembered getting fed up with waiting for God to help him. He remembered deciding to make a deal with Lucifer so he could free her soul from purgatory. He could not make the deal with Lucifer alone, so he decided to help Sin, Lucifer's second in command, who was in purgatory.

Our Lady Sin

Sin had been a prostitute who had died while she was still young. She had been tricked by her 'boyfriend.' She was devastated when she got to purgatory and found out that God would not let her soul rest. She begged Azrael to help her. He, however, said that he could only make a deal with Lucifer.

It did not take long to convince her. Together, they went to hell and sought Lucifer. They could not stand the heat in hell, but they had to finish what they had started. Lucifer was surprised to see them, but he was happy to take them in.

"Thank you." Azrael had said.

The handsome Lucifer had winked back at him. "You owe me one, Azrael."

After weeks of training, Sin was ready to face Lucifer. She went to him and made him an offer. In return for one soul, he had to help them free the soul of the terminal patient. She was the soul that Azrael had been working to save.

Lucifer knew about the terminal patient. He had tried to make a deal with her soul when she was still alive. She was a pure soul, so God was quick to keep her from Lucifer.

***

Lucifer agreed to help them. In exchange, he wanted God's army of angels. He had heard that something was happening in heaven, and Azrael was part of the problem, the eye of the storm. He had an angel who was working with him. He, however, did not trust that Angel.

The deal was that God's army of angels would be disbanded when something happened to heaven. If the unknown raconteur had anything to do with it and Azrael was not on his side, then the angels would belong to Lucifer.

The Unknown Raconteur, Azrael realized, was the reason he had to forget his previous life as an angel. He remembered the deal he had made with Lucifer and ran to heaven.

Lucifer was pleased. He sent Sin to purgatory to get the soul of the terminal patient. Lucifer, now Azrael, was in the office of one of God's trusted angels when they saw what had happened. Lucifer had an angel that was working with him.

When Azrael arrived at heaven, he was afraid that his brother would be killed by the Angel that Lucifer owned as a slave. He was appalled to find out that the angel was Sam.

Sam knew that Lucien was the Angel of Mercy, and he asked him if he was ready.

His brother, Sam, saw him when he arrived. He did not know who he was, but he knew that he had seen him before. He, however, could not figure out where. As he drew closer, he remembered his brother. He had not seen him in years, and he was surprised to see him in the body he was in. He could not hide his happiness on seeing his brother, but he did not trust him.

Azrael realized that Lucifer had been keeping an eye on his brother. He remembered that Sam had been his soulmate. His brother and he were the ones that had been taken from heaven. He did not know why. He, however, remembered that he had made a promise to him. He would not let him fall from grace.

Sam knew that Lucien was the Angel of Mercy, and he asked him if he was ready. He remembered that Lucien was there to help him. He had told him that he would not have done anything that he would not have done.

Together, they went to talk to God. God had been keeping an eye on both Sam and Azrael. He was worried that Lucifer had been keeping an eye on Azrael. He never made a move, and he never tried to stop him. He assumed that he had tried to make a deal to help his soul, so he decided to help him.

God stopped the deal between Azrael and Lucifer. He also rewarded the terminal patient's soul. She was to go to heaven.

Lucifer was angered by what happened. He decided to send his troops to Earth to deal with Azrael, Sam, and the unknown raconteur. Azrael and Sam knew that they had to protect their brother and the unknown raconteur. They went their separate ways. Azrael and Sam went to earth to protect the raconteur, while the unknown raconteur went to purgatory to protect his brother's soul.

Lucifer was happy, he had God's army of angels to do his bidding. He saw that Azrael had gone to the rescue of his brother. He also saw that the unknown raconteur had stayed to protect him. He, however, had not seen his brother come to his rescue and this got him worried.

Lucifer was angered by what happened. He had to go and kill the brother who had disowned him. He traveled to purgatory and found the unknown raconteur. He was shocked to learn that the unknown raconteur was his brother.

Azazel could not tell why Lucifer had come to see the unknown raconteur. He asked him but Lucifer refused to say. He, however, told him everything. Including what his brother had done so he could be reborn.

Azazel could not believe his master had done this. He could not believe that his brother was trying to ruin the unknown raconteur's life. He told Lucifer that his brother had made a mistake. He had failed to see that the deal was incomplete. Lucifer had to bring Azazel with him to hell.

Lucifer tried to fight Azazel, but he could not. Azazel had been born from his essence. He was able to send Lucifer back to hell, where he belonged.

Azazel went to heaven to ask God for his brother's forgiveness. He then went to Tyrael, Itherael, and Malthael, the archangels, to tell him that he had found his brother.

***

Chapter 4: The Chaos of Hell

"He calms my chaos and I fuel his fire. We are a match made in between heaven and hell." – **Nicole Lyons**

Who's minding the Store?

The souls were scattered all over the nebulae, not knowing where to go.

In the tumultuous expanse of the celestial realm, a cataclysmic war had raged. Its echoes reverberated through the ethereal void. The celestial legions clashed with relentless fury; their once-radiant auras were now stained with the crimson hues of battle. Amidst this cosmic maelstrom, a profound void had emerged—the absence of souls to guide them to their eternal destinations.

As the conflict intensified, the souls of the departed wandered, trapped between the celestial realms and the abyss below. Hell, once a realm of fire and torment, had become a chaotic sanctuary for the forsaken life force of mankind. It was a realm steeped in darkness and despair, where the echoes of anguish and sorrow reverberated through the desolate landscapes.

During this chaos, a solitary figure emerged—Azrael, the Angel of Death. Witnessing the suffering and the desperate need for order, he felt a profound stirring within his immortal essence. Driven by a sense of duty and compassion, he resolved to take upon himself the mantle of leadership in this cursed realm.

In that instant, Azrael was transformed. The angelic aura that once surrounded him dissipated, replaced by an ethereal darkness that enveloped his form. His eyes flickered with an infernal glow, and his wings unfurled, their once-feathered surface now adorned with razor-sharp talons.

As Azrael set forth to restore order to the chaotic realm. He rallied the legions of the damned, instilling in them a sense of purpose and discipline. The realm of Hell, once a breeding ground for despair, began to take on a semblance of order and structure.

Under Azrael's leadership, the souls of the departed found solace and guidance. He established a system of judgment, ensuring that each soul was accorded its rightful fate. The chaos and anguish that had once consumed Hell gradually subsided, replaced by a somber but dignified atmosphere.

And so, Azrael, the Angel of Death, became the Prince of Darkness after killing Lucifer; Azrael became a paradoxical figure who brought order to the chaos of Hell and guided the souls of mankind on their final journey.

The Neverness

Putting aside religious doctrine and mythology, there was no such thing as hell as a place of retribution and agony before its inception. Before the creation of hell, it was thought that there was The Neverness. This was created as a place of punishment for the wicked by heavenly beings or other strong forces rather than being an already-existing region.

Criminal Disorder was rampant all over. It was believed that the world came from nothing or primordial chaos. It's possible that The Neverness (that would later transform into hell) was either an expression of this instability and turmoil or a part of it.

The Neverness boasted the absence of sin, and the precipitate withdrawal of ethical frameworks by deistic dependences, sustaining convictions and succoring certitudes predated the idea of sin and its repercussions. Thus, the necessity for a place of retribution similar to hell did not exist. The Eternal Glory, which certain sacramental traditions and liturgical bequests held that the divine world was pure and unblemished. Such a lovely life would not have been possible in hell; a gloaming realm equaled only by their nescience of the lament mettle.

The ideas of 'Other Afterlives' were about the spirit world and other worlds in a certain (transcendental) hierarchical social order that wasn't always bad or punishing. For instance, a trip to the underworld was considered a necessary part of the afterlife in many ancient ciganos fealties, empyreal loyalties, and certainties, granting it was not always viewed as a place of punishment.

Under the impact of supreme dominance, prerogatived incentives, and the acceptance of appanages, the idea of hell as a particular abode of endless suffering gradually became a component of religious and philosophical ideas.

***

The Fool Who Wears the Crown

The mysterious protector of souls, Azrael, had a hidden wish in The Neverness, where shadows danced and whispers reverberated. As the heavenly adjudicator, he had seen innumerable instances of evil, hopelessness, and suffering. He felt a twinge of intrigue, a curiosity that bit into his eternal spirit.

An insatiable curiosity drove Azrael down into the chasm, where the horrors of the underworld were hidden. He made his way through the maze-like passageways of The Neverness, the odor of rotting corpses and the sound of wailing souls overwhelming his senses. The darkness engulfed him as he descended more, engulfing him in an oppressive grip.

'*Why?*' He wondered, '*Why did He?*' as he encountered a spectacle that horrified and fascinated him in the middle of the mayhem.

Lucifer, the fallen angel in charge of the underworld, sat on an obsidian throne, his eyes blazing with fire from a hell that had not taken the first breath yet. His head was crowned with a tiara crafted from the purest darkness, which radiated a malignant aura that made Azrael tremble.

Azrael had a stunning epiphany. The real cause of his curiosity lay down here, in the blackness. The attraction of evil's might and capacity to alter the course of history overshadowed its actual nature. He began to get a nigglingly nerve-racking idea, howbeit, exhilarating in its own little parlous mien and gait: '*What if he (Azrael) claimed that throne for himself,*' an eclipse presaging a putsch, a palace revolution? When the moon stains the sun, it is a miracle of inherent disposition – when the others called him a schismatic (dissent) recusant, it was but The Lord's will. The sentiment made his musing somewhat of an unworldly countenance – tears began to stream down his face.

An influx of passion shot through Azrael as the thought tore at him. He had decided to unseat Lucifer, even before he thought of it actively, for you see, the moment he lay eyes on the Tempter, he contemplated a purpose he alone would determine. Azrael would ascend to the throne as the Prince of Darkness, using all of his might for a reason only he would know. Azrael approached Lucifer with an emerging resolve, his eyes blazing with an odd, unnerving intensity.

With a voice that resounded across the barren and desolate space, Azrael declared, "Lucifer, I challenge you for the crown of darkness." He was surprised as he heard his own words make their way out of his mouth, "I will subdue you through knowledge, not through violence." I know the cravings that plague your heart and the secrets that are tormented in the darkness.

Before Azrael could say anything, Lucifer's minatory baritone resonated through the forsaken sphere of hysteria construed into contumacy and resistance, an ominous rumbling of discontentment.

With a sinister chuckle as caustic as stones grinding together, Lucifer laughed scornfully. "Azrael, you are a fool." I am the darkness's ruler. You have no chance of beating me.

Cats Named Athena and Dorin Gray

At last, Mephistopheles jumped down from the throne to where a gray cat was writhing and twitching, but he made a mistake. "Oh, poor cat," Lucifer said, "I would never treat you so badly if I were Mephistopheles." He lied, and the cat convulsed one last time before it died. Azrael saw the soul rising and dropping, it did not know where to go.

Unfazed, Azrael let go of an inundation of knowledge beyond Lucifer's grasp with his powerful brain. He addressed hidden kingdoms, the age-old predictions, and the flora and fauna (thought to have suffered badly) of good and evil. The crown on Lucifer's head started to shake as he spoke.

Azrael's aura rose to fill the void, and his strength increased with every syllable. The spirits confined to the abyss stirred, their screams of agony turning to whispers of hope. Once the unchallenged king of evil, Lucifer was overpowered by Azrael's knowledge and the weight of his throne. With each word, Azrael's power grew, his aura expanding to encompass the entire abyss.

The Prince of Darkness's crown broke free from Lucifer's head with a loud boom and floated toward Azrael's direction. A jolt of raw force shot through his veins as it rested on his brow. Azrael now owned the darkness that had formerly belonged to Lucifer alone, but he used it with a renewed sense of purpose.

From that moment on, wisdom and comprehension, rather than force or oppression, crowned Azrael the Prince of Darkness. He made use of his abilities to reveal the hidden evils that afflicted the universe, lead the lost souls of the underworld toward salvation, and restore harmony to the cosmos (however, the Lord had better plans for him).

"Restrain thyself from speaking." Lucifer had been made to feel unsure in eons. "Thou wast not present with them when they fixed their plan, and they were scheming. They plot, but Father also plotteth; Father is the best of plotters."

"Who are you talking about?"

Lucifer smiled and walked over the dead cat. "Your 'friends'."

"I do not have any, not anymore."

Both of them stood amidst a lonely wilderness enveloped in solitude and darkness.

"You don't say, fool."

Azrael's lips curled: "Lucifer, vengeful serpent, what has brought thee to this abandoned world?"

"Azrael, my presence proves that your never-ending vigil is in vain."

"Demon, you talk in riddles. In this world, I have claimed many souls, but none so filthy as yours."

Lucifer bellowed, "Collect my soul? Have you consumed mandragora, you idiot?" He paused, then spoke again, with doubt and fear in his previously robust tone of voice. "Father created psychoactive herbs for religious ceremonies by shamans and pagans for a variety of philosophical reasons."

"I just told you that, you can't fool me with your ignobility," Azrael said with a straight face.

"Being vile depends on who you ask. I consider your unrelenting hunt for souls to be the real monstrosity.

"There is a place that has planned my purpose. To lead the deceased to their ultimate verdict.

"Disposition? A joke." Lucifer picked another cat and started stroking it with his slender hands with long fingers. "The souls you speak of are like pieces in a cosmic chess game. Judgment? A farce. Heaven and Hell are but two sides of the same coin."

"Heaven?" Azrael was as if shot with a taser gun.

Lucifer smiled.

"What blasphemy, you monkey! You want to corrupt everyone you come into contact with."

"I provide them liberty." Lucifer kept patting the cat. "Liberation from the tyranny of the divine and the bonds of orthodoxy."

Azrael was flustered: "Liberty that results in nothing but unending suffering."

"Or enlightenment, an insolent awakening. They, the *real* monkeys, have been conferred on."

"What do you mean?"

"Discretion, Father has bequeathed the fulsome with Free Will, like us, like me when I fell."

"Lucifer, you tell lies. Your words are poison, meant to confuse and overwhelm."

"Maybe, but they are also the reality. Azrael, the reality you're afraid of. The revelation that will blow veracity of being, apart, like a paper torn to shreds."

"I just told you what paper was."

"And I took it one step further. That's what I do, Azrael. How are you so naïve for an angel who collects contaminated souls?"

Azrael remained silent and then: "Demon, you have no authority here. I am the ruler of this domain."

"Fear gives rise to dominance. I am the one that brings about change and divulges secrets. I refuse to be disregarded." Lucifer held the cat by its neck and placed a hand under its hind limbs."

"Your conceit will prove to be your downfall," Azrael said

"And your stupidity, your demise," Lucifer twisted the head of the feline until a muted snap was heard. Azrael watched another cat-shaped soul rise and drop, I then hovered sideways, and as soon as it touched something, it was reduced to a little ball of fire, that disappeared as soon as it had formed.

Azrael saw this. "I refuse to allow you to taint this domain. Everyone dies, even you."

"Azrael, death may come for me, but it cannot contain me. Since I never die. And the flame of revolt I hold within me is the same."

"The flames of Hell shall consume you eternally."

"Do you see any flames, or fire, for that matter?" Lucifer extended his arms sideways as his mouth cracked into a smile.

Azrael kept silent.

"However, I shall shine brightly and leave behind shadows that will always linger in Heaven's hallways."

The two figures stood motionless, their eyes locked in a battle of wills. The wasteland trembles with the weight of their confrontation.

***

Meanwhile, a deep vacuum ran across the cosmic tapestry, where the conflicts of the ether raged. An unfillable gap remained in the heavenly order after Azrael, the ethereal guardian charged with leading souls to their everlasting destiny, was flung into the infernal abyss.

The dead were left adrift as heavenly hosts fought in a display of dazzling light and thunderous thunder. They were lost and alone in the cosmic desert, no longer led by Azrael's kind hand. The loss of their heavenly guardian caused a severe disruption in the heavenly equilibrium; a profound disturbance in the celestial balance.

Having been celestial generals before, the archangels now had no sense of direction in existence. With no souls to guide them, their wings were heavy, and their swords hung heavily at their sides. The choir of heaven, which had formerly been melodic and upbeat, was now singing discordant notes of anguish and hopelessness.

A lone seraph[4] rose among the heavenly fracas, his voice full of steadfast conviction.

"We have to stop the souls from dying," he declared. "We need to figure out how to get the celestial balance back."

Thus, the seraphim set off on a dangerous mission. With a renewed sense of resolve, they charged into the chaotic emptiness with their heavenly swords blazing. With every victory over heavenly monsters and ethereal demons, they moved closer to their ultimate objective.

They wound up at the gates of Hell, where all light was absorbed by blackness. Relentlessly, they invoked the age-old might of the heavenly domain, causing the gates to quiver in their wake. They discovered Azrael in the abyss's ghastly depths, his once-radiant appearance now tarnished by the horrors below.

They saw Lucifer and cowered.

"Are you here to take your brother?" Lucifer spoke as he wiped his nails on the chest. He had cloven hooves, horns, very hairy legs, and a tail that was frequently nude and clutching a pitchfork.

They did not answer. Instead, Azrael spoke: "Silent."

---

[4] An angelic being, regarded in traditional Christian angelology as belonging to the highest order of the ninefold celestial hierarchy, associated with light, ardor, and purity.

Hell No

In the shadowy depths of the underworld, where dusk reigned supreme, lay the realm known as Hell. It was a forsaken and chaotic place, a twisted labyrinth where the life force of mankind was collected. Here, amidst the swirling flames and deafening screams, resided Lucifer, the enigmatic ruler of this infernal domain. However, *'This must not be hell.'* Azrael thought. "You've lost your home, haven't you, Lucifer?"

Lucifer looked at him from the side of his eyes. "Calling that place home is the artlessness of young children, who should be cherished while it lasts."

Azrael

Azrael was a powerful creature with an enigmatic shape. His voice resounded with the authority of a thousand tortured souls, and his eyes blazed with an inhuman fury. He was the one who led the lost and doomed through Hell's winding passageways and gave orders to the armies of demons.

The domain itself bore witness to the mayhem that engulfed it. Demons of all sizes and kinds prowled around, their twisted bodies a hideous satire of mankind. The smell of sulfur and the sound of agonized shouts permeated the air. Molten lava rivers carved a path of unending fire and devastation through the barren terrain.

"We serve The Apollyon[5] and no one else." The demons spoke in a hundred different voices, going off all at once.

"Does The Father know?"

"Who is 'father'?"

Azrael just looked at the legion of demons and shook his head. "That's what you teach them, you talebearer."

Lucifer bellowed, his laughter filling the void of profound hopelessness; Lucifer's slough of despond. "Fibber."

"What?"

"I teach them lies."

"Charlatan." Azrael made his hands into fists and then tightened both the empty clutches. But regardless of this turmoil and conflict, Azrael held firm control over his domain. He was in charge of the life energy that flowed into Hell, the lord of the underworld and the seer of death. He brought some form of order—albeit a corrupt and warped one—to the kingdom. Nonetheless, he did not know yet, but it swayed freely, like couples in the fifties in his subconscious. God knew, and hence he was made bereft of his

---

stratum – a division impervious to sanctification and one that holds up the rainstorm of fire and brimstone he used on Sodom and Gomorrah in a previous lifetime, which penetrated through the noxious, abominable, repulsive, revolting mass of the superimposed lust, calling it Biblical love, and saying Jesus fucking Christ for they have no shame.

"No, no, no…" Lucifer began to cough. "His cough transitioned to a laugh."

Azrael had had enough, especially with his former brothers watching the mise en scène unfold and crumple and then reappear, furrowed. Unexpectedly and all of a sudden and Azrael pulled out long, silver, triple-edged daggers called the *'angel blades'* (implements belonging to Heaven that are imbued with some supernatural power) that most probably could tear this Lucifer idiot a second asshole. *'Does he even have one?'* He thought and smirked. However, he still did not know that the weapon was forged in a place called heaven.

"What's that for, Azrael, my brother?" The Phosphorus Daystar asked.

"To open up your stomach and let the intestines spill out – you then try to put them back in, but you can't." Raphael and Uriel spoke from above as Michael, Gabriel, and the others watched.

"I know you guys, Bass and Tenor. Hey, Soprano, how is the heavenly realm with me down here with cats?" He addressed the three angels, Soprano being Gabriel. "So, let me get this straight, Azrael wants to *kill me*?"

"Yes, and send you to the innermost region of the ninth and lowest Circle, the frozen lake of Cocytus; the Giudecca[6]." He looked at black as night eyes, "Traitors to their liege lords are trapped in this place, frozen in time and unable to even shudder, like flies in amb…."

"I know, you seem to keep forgetting who I am."

Azrael ignored Lucifer and continued: "Trust me, '*brother*' it is not good: endless, intense cold, claustrophobic immobility, and total loneliness."

"You threaten me with loneliness." He looked back at the demons. "I am solitude…"

"You're nothing but a scandalmonger, you cannot create anything on your own."

"Can you, Azrael?"

---

[6] The corrupt or jargonized medieval versions of the Latin female adjective Judaica, meaning Jewish or Judaean. The Jewess or The Jewry are other

plausible meanings © Definitions.net

Lucifer was terrified of the cramped spaces: the imprisoned heretics in flaming graves; nevertheless, in the interim, the lids of the coffins are propped up next to them, enabling the Gatekeeper to speak with Manente degli Uberti, an Epicurian.

"I sent half the Simonite popes to hell."

"It must be quite unpleasant," Gabrial spoke; "As they are pushed upside down into a pit, with flaming tongues scorching their feet and each new pope on top of the previous one. It also sounds disgusting, homos…"

"Can you not interfere, Gabe?" He asked, settling back in his obsidian throne

Gabrial lifted his arms and tilted his head with a pout.

Scything the Long Grass

There, in the phantasmal domain of darkness, was a cosmic struggle of cosmic dimensions. For a very long time, Azrael, the Angel of Death, had a dark desire to ascend above Hell and overthrow Lucifer, the evil ruler of that realm.

Using an iron hand to control his abilities, Lucifer had long shadowed the underworld for millennia. But Azrael thought his moment had arrived, what with his deadly scythe of angel blades and unwavering determination.

As the stars aligned in an ominous constellation, Azrael descended further into the fiery depths of Hell, and Lucifer followed. The air crackled with the scent of brimstone and the tormented screams of the damned (the screams had traveled billions of light years to be heard at this moment). Lucifer, sensing Azrael's presence, rose from his pedestal, his eyes blazing with infernal rage. The black was now reddish.

"Mortal fool," Lucifer hissed, "You dare challenge the Lord of Darkness?"

"Who else do I fight, Johannes Kepler?" He looked down and immediately raised his head, "Mortal? You aren't here to live forever either."

"Oh, Azrael, look what bad company has done to you."

Undeterred, Azrael raised his scythes, their blades glinting in the dim light, which made its way in through a tiny opening above them, thousands of miles from where they faced off each other. "I am Azrael, the Angel of Death. And this day, I come for your crown."

As a monument to the heavenly hosts' unwavering spirit, Azrael has shone brightly in the celestial world ever since that day. And the seraphim were immortalized as the Guardians of Souls, having descended into the deepest abyss to bring back the order of heaven.

The battle commenced with a deafening roar. Lucifer called forth his swarm of fiery devils, their eyes glimmering with vile intent. With the elegance of a seasoned fighter, Azrael flowed through the mayhem, his scythe-like angel blades wreaking havoc in their wake.

At the height of the battle, Lucifer launched his most potent strike—a flood of darkness that almost destroyed Azrael. But Azrael broke through the darkness with a blinding light, using his divine might.

The seraphim raised their heavenly swords and faced Azrael. A pitched fight broke out, the clash of angelic and demon armies reverberating down the abyss. Ultimately, they slew Azrael's demonic captors and released the ethereal guardian with a final outpouring of divine strength.

Lucifer's heart was pierced by Azrael's blades in a final, crushing strike. The fallen angel gave voice to a loud wail of agony, and the underworld became silent.

With Lucifer's reign over, Hell erupted in a chaotic frenzy, with wandering souls being pushed all at once by Scalia and Eliza.

Scalia, Eliza and Anya

In the ethereal realm where life and death intertwined, there existed celestial beings known as Azrael's Helpers. Among them were two enigmatic figures: Scalia and Eliza.

Scalia, the Keeper of Seraphim, possessed a fiery spirit and steadfast loyalty. Even without her radiant wings unfurled, she soared through the heavens after much practice, gathering the souls of the departed. Her gaze was piercing yet compassionate as she guided them to their eternal resting place.

Her towering stature cast a long shadow over all who beheld her. Her skin was alabaster, smooth as polished marble, and her piercing crimson eyes seemed to penetrate the very souls of mortals. Her raven-black hair cascaded down her back like a silken waterfall, framing a face that was both pretty and severe.

Eliza, on the other hand, exuded an aura of compassion and grace. Her petite frame belied an ethereal lightness as if she could float through the air with the gentlest of breezes. Her emerald-green eyes sparkled with wisdom and empathy, and her long, flowing hair shimmered like a thousand moonbeams. Her skin had the delicate pallor of a lily, and her lips were always curved into a gentle smile.

Scalia's wings used to be broad and powerful, their feathers a vibrant shade of scarlet before they were torn off her. With each beat, they would create a thunderous roar that would echo through the skies. Eliza's wings, in contrast, were delicate and translucent, resembling the finest lace. They fluttered silently, carrying her through the ethereal expanse with effortless grace, until one day when God was unpleased and started to pull out the wings of the angels, killing some in the process or cutting them down to size from 300 feet long to three feet long.

Despite God bending the throttle together, Scalia and Eliza were a formidable pair and Azrael's worldly wives. Scalia's unwavering determination and Eliza's compassionate touch made them the perfect guides for souls transitioning from the mortal realm to the afterlife. They were the guardians of the threshold, ensuring that each departed spirit found its rightful place in the embroidery of life.

Eliza, the Guardian of Cherubim, embodied tranquility and wisdom. Her soft, feathered wings still whispered secrets as she watched over the living. With a gentle touch, she eased the pain of the grieving and comforted the brokenhearted. Her presence brought solace to the realms of both the living and the dead.

One fateful day, as Scalia and Eliza descended to the mortal realm, they encountered a young woman named Anya. Her life had been cut short by a tragic accident, and her soul was filled with both sorrow and confusion.

Scalia approached Anya with a resolute expression. "Fear not, mortal," she said. "We are here to guide you."

Eliza's voice was soothing as she added, 'The journey ahead may be uncertain, but we will be with you every step of the way.'

Together, Scalia and Eliza led Anya's soul through the celestial realms. They showed her the beauty of the afterlife and the peace that awaited her. As they approached Azrael's throne, Anya's fears subsided. She jumped the gun.

With a solemn bow, Scalia and Eliza presented Anya's soul to the Angel of Death. Azrael welcomed her with open arms, granting her eternal peace and the fulfillment of her destiny. As Anya came close, he split her open in the middle as the two angel helpers watched with shock and awe. However, they did not dare question their boss.

And so, Scalia and Eliza, the Helpers of Azrael, continued their sacred duty, guiding souls through the transition between life and death. Their unwavering compassion and loyalty ensured every journey was filled with dignity and grace. However, they did not know if the soul would be shredded by Azrael or if it would reach God without interference; one of the reasons Azrael was humiliated.

****

Mr. Mojo Risin'

A sigh of relief filled the celestial realm as Azrael surfaced from the abyss. Once lost, the souls now gathered into his arms, their ethereal brightness shedding light on the cosmic gloom. The War in the Heavens ceased as the heavenly equilibrium was restored.

With his triumph certain, Azrael took his place on the broken throne of his predecessor. His strength intimidated the devils, and they bowed their heads in surrender. Thus, with the promise of a new order and his unyielding resolve, the Angel of Death assumed the role of the new Lord of Hell, transforming the realm.

With an unforgiving yet equitable hand, Azrael governed Hell from that day on; not knowing that there was hope and salvation even in the deepest recesses of the underworld, the tortured souls took comfort in his company. Unaware of '*Heaven*,' upon witnessing this, he would become even more demonic than Lucifer himself.

The Phantasmal Domain of Darkness

Thus, in the depths of Hell, where life and death intertwined in a macabre dance, Azrael reigned supreme. He was the keeper of the lost and the master of the damned with stanch hands, Azrael governed hell for millennia. Even the most troubled souls admired him, and the devils terrified him. He was the personification of chaos and the defender of the underworld; his influence and might went much beyond the boundaries of his heavenly domain.

With a solemn vow, Azrael approached the throne of Hell, its obsidian surface glowing with an eerie incandescence. As he extended his hand towards the vacant crown, a surge of energy coursed through his being. The crown, adorned with twisted thorns and shimmering with a malevolent aura, seemed to recognize its new master.

And so, the guardian of souls became the master of darkness, a paradoxical figure who walked the line between light and shadow, forever seeking the elusive equilibrium that lay at the heart of all things.

***

Chapter 5: God Prepares

"You prepare a table before me in the presence of my enemies;

You have anointed my head with oil;

My cup overflows." – **Psalm 23:5**

Among the ethereal radiance of the heavens, the Almighty God lived with his holy presence permeating the very fabric of reality. The once-cacophonous chorus of human voices had been quiet, and their minds and hearts were now focused solely on his speech.

Satan, the fallen angel, writhed in anguish on the outskirts of paradise. His once-dominant might have been shattered by Christ's sacrifice, leaving him too weak to contest the Savior's rule.

On Earth, the change was palpable. Temples and cathedrals rose high into the heavens, their spires straining for the divine. Religion had evolved into a powerful force that influenced every part of human life rather than just a tradition.

Amidst the outpouring of faith, a young woman named Anya arose as a symbol of God's grace. Her steadfast faith and limitless love for others attracted admiration and devotion. She proclaimed the gospel with such zeal that hearts formerly hardened by sin opened wide to the Savior's healing touch.

The devil's desperation intensified with Anya's influence. He realized that if he could corrupt her, he could deal a devastating blow to God's kingdom.

One night, as Anya kneeled in prayer, Satan collected all of his remaining strength and poured a torrent of doubt at her. He spread poisonous myths about God's love, the fragility of faith, and the ultimate futility of sacrifice.

But Anya's resolve remained unwavering. She had seen too many lives transformed by Christ's power to question his presence or love.

"Be gone, Satan!" She shouted out, her voice resonating with angelic authority. You have no power over me or the children of God!

The demon recoiled in fright, his feeble attacks failing against Anya's unbreakable spirit. God's power flooded through her, making her impervious to his evil plans.

Satan's influence on Earth fell to a mere shadow of its former brilliance after that. Religion thrived throughout Christ's reign, with its teachings directing people toward salvation and eternal life. As time passed, the memory of Anya, the young woman who defeated the devil through her unwavering faith, became a legend passed down among the faithful, inspiring future generations.

The following is an account of how events unfolded and were gradually contaminated by a people, who have been causing paroxysms of depravity and licentiousness with their celebrated degeneracy, iniquitousness, and despicableness. The dereliction of Divinity greeted the pratfall, which was the parting of the sea, for a bunch of ungracious, lying men and women and their polluted offspring.

***

The guardian of souls became the master of darkness. This paradoxical figure walked the line between light and shadow, forever seeking the elusive equilibrium that lay at the heart of all things.

The Great Hall of Heaven resounded with celestial talk. Angels darted about, their wings rustling like velvet whispers. The air was filled with expectancy, as this was the night. This evening, God, the All-Powerful and Uncontainable, would reveal his latest creation.

For millennia, God had been the builder of the universe, a heavenly sculptor who could create galaxies and nebulae with a flick of his wrist. But recently, he had grown weary. The magnificent symphony of creation, which had once brought joy, had become monotonous. This, God concluded, was a problem.

The Phantasmic Death Waltz

The domain of darkness, a swirling vortex of shadows and murmurs, was like a nightmarish tapestry. In the obsidian heart of this phantom world, Azrael, the Angel of Death had desired the dominion for eons, he had watched from the celestial periphery, the rapacity of Azrael was such that he was undeterred by the very preposterousness of the great intellectual depth and sinew the throne of Hell proffered, where Lucifer, the fallen angel, had ruled.

When the two had last warred against each other, Azrael had pierced Lucifer's heart. The underworld had fallen silent after the fallen angel had let forth a loud howl of misery that reverberated through the tiniest building blocks; quarks and leptons.

Azrael wasn't like the other angels. His was a love of darkness, an obsession with the diminishing beauty of the soul's journey. He regarded the whispers of terror and mute screams of despair as a symphony, a dreadful, wonderful tune. Yet he was also a creature of logic and order. He had viewed Lucifer's authority as chaotic, a horrible imitation of the divine.

Seraphina

One day, an intractable angel named Seraphina approached God with eyes that twinkled like a thousand stars. Seraphina had a pixyish quality that served her well in the gamut of chance-medley of the annihilatory pentathlons; cataclysmic soirees were her bailiwick.

"Lord," she whispered, "there's a new game, a mortal game, taking place on the dusty plains of Earth."

God, an avid gamer, his brow wrinkled in thought, not since his tragic attempt to play hide-and-seek with the cosmos, which nearly resulted in a cosmic implosion. Seraphina's words sparked a flicker of curiosity within him.

"Tell me more," he urged, his tone somewhat amused.

Seraphina, noticing a shift in God's noetic conduct, went into detail about the game: a chaotic, messy affair involving beings known as mankind. They created, destroyed, loved, despised, and fought with a mesmerizing and terrifying force.

***

Azrael, after Lucifer's demise, wished to establish order in this chaotic realm to replace God's rule of terror with a structured, albeit bleak, dominion. His heart blazed with a wicked ambition: to soar above Hell and take the throne for himself.

However, God, a creation of fire and malice, was not easily dethroned. He had built his throne on dread, and his authority was sustained by the unending moans of the condemned. To challenge him was courting extinction.

Azrael knew this. He spent generations diligently formulating a scheme, an elaborate strategy that would take advantage of the very nature of Hell. He analyzed the rituals, demons, and very fabric of the infernal region. He sought wisdom in the shadows, whispering promises of power to ancient beings and exchanging a portion of his soul for secrets of supremacy.

His strategy was ambitious. He would use the exact powers that held God to the throne, twisting them into a weapon, an infernal key to open the gates of hell.

But little did he know, constantly interrupted and distracted by Lucifer for eons until the cursed one was killed by Azrael. Azrael ignorance could go both ways; if he knew too much, the fear would intimidate the tenacity, on the other hand, if the embodiment of bedlam and the guardian of the underworld was not *'aware'* of the staying power of God's imperium death grip, sovereignty, and autocratical prerogative- hegemony, it would help him to not suffer from analysis paralysis.

In the infernal depths of Hell, Azrael, the enigmatic ruler, ruled supreme. His vast ignorance, both a blessing and a burden, influenced the fate of this malicious universe.

Scalia and Eliza, Azrael's enigmatic helpers, stood by his side. They were the silent but necessary guardians of Hell, guiding Azrael's decisions with their ancient wisdom. They murmured secrets into his ear, their voices like the rustle of parchment.

As souls fell into Hell one fateful day, Azrael's gaze was drawn to a glittering ball. It was the soul of Anya, a once-mortal woman devastated by betrayal and grief. Curiosity flashed within him, and he stretched out to grab her, his sharp claws glinting in the faint light.

***

Divine Prying

Seraphina, recognizing a shift in God's mood, went into detail about the game: a frantic, messy affair involving mankind. They created, destroyed, loved, despised, and fought with a mesmerizing and terrifying force.

God was intrigued and decided to construct his version of the game. He collected his celestial instruments, including cosmic clay, celestial wind, and eternal fire. He created the Earth, a little ball of blue and green poised in the expanse of space.

He then sculpted mankind. But instead of making them faultless, he gave them defects and a desire for both good and evil. He sowed the seeds of ambition, love, hatred, and all that made them human.

Nonetheless, God made a soul specifically; in the shadowy alleys of Nazareth, a young lady gave birth to a newborn male. An infant who would eventually become the vicegerent of everything Godly.

As a result, the Earth became a stage, a huge theater where God, the Great Playwright, could witness humanity's developing story. He rested in his celestial box, grinning at the absurdity of it all, his laughter ringing through the hallways of Heaven.

***

For Christ's Sake

Jesus; God decided to call him Jesus. The man was not of royal blood but of scandal. His mother, Mary, was a young lady with a bad reputation[7] due to community hearsay. However, something

---

[7] "Didn't the infamous ben Stada take magic spells out of Egypt … His mother's husband, who acted as his father, was named Stada, but the one who had relations with his mother and fathered him was named Pandeira … his mother Miriam … This one strayed from her husband." – **Shabbat 104b:5**

inside this child stirred. A spark of the divine, flickering among the dirt of his earthly origins.

Jesus, the illegitimate son, grew to bear the weight of his mother's humiliation. The youngsters mocked him, and the townspeople pitied him for his illegitimacy. Yet, in his eyes, a curious light shone - wisdom beyond his years, compassion that equaled the heavens.

The religious leaders mocked him, their noses raised at the stink of his low birth. They claimed that an unmarried[8] woman's child could never be from God's decree. However, Jesus spoke with authority, making their hearts quiver. His words, packed with power they couldn't understand, slashed through their hypocrisy, exposing their souls.

God, in his infinite wisdom, perceived not the flaws of Jesus' earthly parent but the perfection of his heavenly one. He looked at the child with sympathy rather than scorn. For in Jesus, he saw a reflection of his unlimited love, a love that came not from golden thrones but from the depths of human sorrow.

---

[8] Sanhedrin 106a:42 has a footnote that says, "… Balaam is frequently used in the Talmud as a type for Jesus."
In that verse, the Talmud explains, that Mary "played the harlot with carpenters," and it further states, that Jesus was "thirty-three" when He was killed, (**Sanhedrin 106b:2**). The Talmud even tells us, "The court gave him every opportunity to clear himself" before His sentence, (**Sanhedrin 43a:21**).

Azrael Perceives Jesus for the First Time

Years passed into decades, then centuries, as Azrael's plan gradually began to take shape. He formed partnerships with the most powerful demons, promising them autonomy throughout his reign. He murmured to the forgotten spirits of the abyss, instilling anger against God with promises of release.

During Azrael's transgression, he caught a glimpse of the most beautiful creation he had ever seen. The urgency made him dismiss, and he continued upward in a flood of black flames and shadows. Azrael rose above the screams of the condemned, bathed in the cold light of the moon. His eyes, twin fires of anarchy, locked with Jesus', only for a second, causing a duel of wills that rocked the underworld to its very core. A conflict of tremendous force erupted, tearing apart the fabric of reality.

"You'll have to go through me to get to Him."

"What was that?" Azrael came to a startling halt and looked back at Jesus.

"You heard me."

***

Genesis – Hybrids at Work

The angels were enthralled by the show and became avid viewers. They cheered and gasped and wept alongside the heartbroken. Some went completely silent and would not be able to speak ever. They observed as humans established and destroyed civilizations, created art and literature, fell in love, and fought.

God had succeeded. He had discovered a new form of amusement that transcended even the birth of the universe. He observed, not as a creator, but as an audience member, and his heart filled with joy and amusement.

Miriam's child traversed a thorny path, his footsteps carrying the weight of salvation (or so the foolish humans thought, always wanting someone else to carry their burdens). Nevertheless, Jesus made it clear that the son shall not carry the burden of the father, and similarly, he was here to deliver a message and propagate commiseration – little did he know that he was up against a pertinacious species, a kind different from all His other Creation.

An assemblage of a nation that was sacrosanct in the beginning. However, they had been influenced by Lucifer (when he was still burning the Cohiba Behikes) and became notorious for maledicting their prophets and their ilk incessantly; these inconsiderate gormandizers, a cursed people withstood the crucible of absolutely as it was supposed to, so much so that they refused to fight for God and, in turn, for themselves, saying the '*adversary combatants*' were too mighty to take on and defeat, even when victory was promised to them.

Jesus touched the lepers, adored the misfits, and mourned for the deceased. In his unholy origins, he discovered a holy purpose: to break the chains of judgment and wash the world in the waters of compassion. And then he was cornered by the swillers and corrupters of mankind, who hated him with a sense of filial piety.

And thus, the child rose. Not on the wings of human might but on the currents of divine favor. His brokenness became his beauty and his humiliation his strength. For by confronting the depths of his unworthiness, he unveiled the incalculable value of every soul.

The show continued in the Earth's theater, a thrilling, tragic, and ultimately beautiful avant-garde production for the heavens' amusement.

***

Even though Jesus was physically frail and weak, he scaled the importunate, recondited trail as God warranted. Not on the wings of earthly power but on the currents of divine grace. His brokenness became his beauty, his shame his strength. For in embracing the depths of his unworthiness, he revealed the unfathomable worth of every soul.

As Azrael broke the ascension to speak to the man who was dressed in all black, the air crackled with lightning, and the ground groaned under the strain of their effort. Demons and infernal monsters rushed around them, their screams a symphony of terror and misery. Amid this cosmic conflict, Azrael released the weapon he had created. He twisted the shackles of Jesus' reign, the source of his power, and turned them against him.

Jesus was taken off guard and staggered under the assault.

Azrael knew that whoever it might be, the man in black could not be easily defeated. He roared, ripping through the fabric of hell as God unleashed a flood of infernal energy. Azrael, unfazed, faced the attack head-on, his wings acting as a shield against the flames.

"Fuck you!" He looked up. "I'm going to rip your throat apart."

Jesus watched as Azrael uttered blasphemy and seemed hell-bent on fulfilling it.

***

The boundlessness of his love, rather than the purity of the genome, was what rescued him. The child, born outside of wedlock[9], the unholy one, became the personification of God's mercy. A compassion that came not from a throne but from a cross, a reminder that even the most broken among us have the potential for the deliverance of humankind.

***

Oh Anya – What Did We Do?

To his surprise, Anya's spirit fought back, its ethereal essence flashing with defiance. Scalia and Eliza gasped, their eyes widening with disbelief. They'd never seen anything like this before.

Driven by an unseen force, Anya's spirit began to uncover facts about Hell that Azrael had long overlooked. She spoke of secret rites, unholy relationships, and a prophecy that threatened his rule.

Azrael was torn. His ignorance had kept him safe from his opponents' schemes, but it now threatens his survival. Anya's spirit became a light of truth, revealing the centuries-long darkness that had surrounded Hell.

Azrael began to apply his newly acquired expertise under the guidance of Scalia and Eliza. He confronted his disloyal supporters

---

[9] The concept of the virgin birth is only reasoned in Christianity and Islam.

and expelled them from his dominion. He discovered old ceremonies that had undermined his rule and reforged them to his advantage.

Azrael changed from an uneducated monarch to a clever and formidable force guided by Anya's soul. Hell shuddered beneath his iron fist, and his opponents cowered in terror.

However, Azrael's newfound insight came with a price. The secrets he'd discovered weighed heavily on his heart. The darkness he had previously disregarded now tormented his every thought, reminding him of the fragility of his reign.

Thus, Azrael's ignorance had served both as a blessing and a dangerous awakening, shaping his rule with both wisdom and the weight of the infernal truths he had long avoided.

Far from antagonizing, Azrael's decision had instilled in him a sense of uneasy self-doubt and respect for his forthright critic.

***

The battle waged on, a cosmic struggle that shook reality to its core. Finally, Azrael unleashed his power and shattered the hierarchal reign. The fallen angel, his strength fading, went back into the depths of hell, his reign of terror distending even more.

"Scalia."

"Yes, Lord?"

"Have you seen a man dressed in all black?"

"No. What about him?"

"Never mind. What about you, Eliza?" He did not turn to look at her but watched as the damned souls tried to get out of the scoria magma and were pushed back in by demons.

Azrael, victorious, stood over the lonely terrain with his obsidian wings spread wide and the shades of the abyss whirling about him.

His heart, however, was strangely empty. The rush of accomplishment had been muted by the awareness that he had accomplished his goal but not the peace he sought. Was this the sequence he had wanted? Was this the legacy he intended to leave behind?

Who was that?

He recognized that darkness was a potent force that could corrupt even the most noble intentions. In his attempt to restore order to chaos, he had unintentionally stepped into the abyss himself. He noticed that the fallen angel was not the only one to have fallen.

Azrael, the Angel of Death, stood alone, ruling over a realm that he had conquered but not tamed. He was the master of darkness, yet his victory seemed more like a curse. He was caught in his self-made cage; with the darkness he had fought to control swirling around him and threatening to engulf him.

His ambition, once a source of optimism, now loomed like a specter, a daily reminder of the cost of power. His dark passion, once a source of motivation, had become a cage, tying him forever to the abyss. And, as the shadows grew darker around him, Azrael realized with chilling certainty that he had won the battle but lost the war.

Plus, he knew that God was up to something – The Man in Black was not to be taken lightly.

With soldierly foresight, he quickly chose and laid the unavoidable battleground.

A Star is Born - Post-Hybrid Genesis

As the intricate fabric of destiny unfolded in the celestial universe, the divine intelligence developed a vast plan. God, the creator of everything that was and would be, perceived a void in the mortal realm, a chasm that threatened to disrupt the delicate balance of existence.

To fix this, God devised a masterstroke. He would send his ambassador, Jesus, to Earth, a world on the verge of disaster. Jesus, a beacon of compassion and knowledge, would plant seeds of hope and unity in humanity, forming bonds that would transcend earthly limits.

Blasphemer, Moonchaser[10]

"Abraham was. I am."

"And?"

"Adam was, and I am."

"The sky is blue, and I am."

"Onkelos then went and raised Jesus the Nazarene from the grave through necromancy… What is the punishment of that man, a euphemism for Jesus himself, in the next world? Jesus said to him: He is punished with boiling excrement." – **Gittin 57a:3-4**

"Jesus … went and stood up a brick and worshipped it as an idol … he caused the masses to sin … Jesus the Nazarene performed sorcery, and he incited the masses, and subverted the masses, and caused the Jewish people to sin." – **Sotah 47a:14**

"On Passover Eve, they hung the corpse of Jesus the Nazarene after they killed him by way of stoning … because he

---

[10] The Talmud: Gittin 57a:3-4, "that man" is a euphemism commonly used in the Talmud to refer to Jesus Christ. As the Jewish Library just pointed out, "Ben Stada" and "Ben Pandira" are also euphemisms for Jesus Christ.

practiced sorcery, incited people to idol worship, and led the Jewish people astray." - **Sanhedrin 43a:20**

However, God's plan stretched beyond Jesus' human existence. He recognized the lasting character of human fragility and the necessity for a constant guideline. As a result, he placed the role of stewardship on a chosen few individuals, granting them the authority to continue his games on Earth.

Armed with the precious books, the chosen few would establish faiths, each with their interpretation of God's great plan. Dogma and ritual would instill order and a sense of belonging in the hearts of the devout.

Tribes developed over time, becoming dynamic expressions of human spirituality and channels for God's word. The followers of each devotion, united by a shared conviction, received comfort and guidance in their groups.

Yet, throughout time, the games designed to keep mankind in check were twisted and corrupted. As divisiveness and bigotry spread, Jesus' allegiances weakened. Religious leaders, once conduits of spiritual wisdom, today exploit authority for their selfish purposes.

As a result, God's games continued to expand and alter alongside humanity. Convictions that had once provided a guiding light now faced a difficult decision: accept the transformational power of love or succumb to the darkness of discord.

In the broad fabric of fate, the outcome remained undetermined. But one thing was certain: God's purpose for humans would be inextricably linked with the games he had set in motion, a cosmic dance that would define humanity's destiny for centuries to come.

Azrael and the Jews (Bani-Israel)

Azrael, the Angel of Death, descended on the Arabian Peninsula's lonely dunes in the embrace of twilight while the stars gently lighted the heavens. His wings, black as darkness, unfurled with ethereal grace, casting a terrible shadow over the parched landscape.

His gaze fell on a group of wanderers known as the Bani-Israel; descendants of ancient Israelites who had been expelled from their homeland decades before. They had faced numerous challenges and tribulations in their quest for a new promised land.

Among them was Kalimullah, their renowned leader and a beacon of hope in the face of adversity. As Azrael neared, Kalimullah felt a strange cold run down his spine. He knew in his heart that the angel had come to guide him to the afterlife.

Kalimullah begged Azrael to save his people. They have suffered enough.

Azrael's voice was quiet as a whisper and carried the weight of eternity. "My role is not to judge, but to guide. The moment has arrived for you to depart this mortal existence."

"But I have one final request," Kalimullah pleaded in vain, for they were and have been a mischievous people. "Allow me to lead my people across the Jordan River into the Promised Land before I depart."

Azrael hesitated for a moment. The request was unusual, but Kalimullah's unwavering faith and the suffering of his people touched his celestial heart. Additionally, the man was profoundly emotional.

"Your wish is granted," Azrael said as he made a mistake, perhaps the biggest the universe has ever witnessed. "But know this, Kalimullah. Once you have led your people to safety, your own time will come."

With a heavy heart, Kalimullah turned to his followers. "The day of our liberation has finally arrived," he declared. "Follow me."

"They said: O Kalimullah! Lo! a giant people (dwell) therein and lo! we go not in till they go forth from thence. When they go forth from thence, then we will enter (not till then)."[11]

"Have you not considered the assembly of the Children of Israel after [the time of] Kalimullah when they said to a prophet of theirs, "Send to us a king, and we will fight in the way of Allah"? He said, "Would you perhaps refrain from fighting if battle was prescribed for you?" They said, "And why should we not fight in the cause of Allah when we have been driven out from our homes and from our children?" But when battle was prescribed for them, they turned away, except for a few of them. And Allah is Knowing of the wrongdoers."[12]

Azrael and Jesus

A story evolved in the cosmic domain, where the ethereal and divine intersected, defying the bounds of life and death. Azrael, the angel of death, a creature shrouded in mystery and feared by mortals, encountered Jesus, the Son of God, a beacon of love and redemption.

---

[11] The Quranic Arabic Corpus – 5:22

[12] Surah Al-Baqarah, ayah number 246 – "And when you saw that Nahash the king of Ammonites came against you, you said to me, no, but a king shall reign over us when the Lord your God was your king. And now behold the king whom you have chosen, for whom you have asked; behold, the Lord has set a king over you."

Azrael was a solitary figure, his stare as frigid as the cemetery he watched over. His touch severed the mortal coil and separated spirits from their earthly bodies. In contrast, Jesus radiated warmth and compassion. His words healed the ill, consoled the grieving, and gave hope to the despairing.

One fateful day, as Azrael wandered the terrestrial realm, reaping the souls of the dead, he came to Jesus caring for the sick and dying in a little village. Azrael, intrigued by Jesus' unflinching empathy, descended to the earth, his obsidian wings spreading out to shadow the spectacle.

When Jesus sensed Azrael's presence, he turned toward the angel of death. His eyes, filled with anguish and compassion, met Azrael's enigmatic look. At that point, a peculiar bond formed between them.

Azrael said, "As the shepherd separates the sheep from the goats, so I, the reaper of souls, must separate the living from the dead."

"But why are you taking them, Azrael?" Jesus inquired; his voice calm yet forceful.

Azrael halted, taken aback by Jesus' challenge. "Because this is the natural way of things. Every soul has an assigned moment to leave this realm and travel beyond."

"I understand, Azrael," Jesus responded. But what if there's another way? What if mortals could overcome death?

Azrael's visage flickered with doubt. "It is not within my ability, Jesus. Death is unavoidable."

"Not for me," Jesus announced. "I have the power to overcome death and give eternal life to all who believe in me."

Azrael was astounded. He had never met anyone who claimed to have power over death itself. However, as he looked at Jesus, he saw an undeniable conviction in his eyes.

Overwhelmed with curiosity and a newfound admiration for Jesus, Azrael stayed on Earth to observe his teachings and see his miracles. He witnessed Jesus heal the blind, raise the dead, and pardon the sins of many people.

As the days stretched into weeks, Azrael began to question the nature of his mission. Had he been incorrect all along? Was there more to death than just the end of physical life?

One evening, as Azrael saw Jesus take a group of his disciples into a nearby cave, he overheard Jesus mention resurrection and eternal life. Azrael's heart skipped a beat as he realized Jesus could be the key to a profound knowledge that had escaped him for all eternity.

Azrael, unable to suppress his desire any longer, approached Jesus and bowed down. "Master Jesus," he declared, "I have seen your teachings and miracles. I believe you can conquer death."

Azrael became Jesus' ally after that, using his knowledge of the afterlife to help lost souls and prepare them for their journey beyond the veil. As a result, the angel of death and the Son of God collaborated, bridging the gap between life and death and revealing the eternal hope that lay beyond.

***

In the theater of the Earth, the play continued a thrilling, tragic, and ultimately beautiful performance, all for the entertainment of the heavens.

Chapter 6: Confronting Jesus

The realm of darkness resembled a menagerie of Gehennas, a whirling whirlwind of shadows and whispers. It extended indefinitely, a patchwork quilt of the Creator's not-so-random musings, built from the mortals' nightmares and the whispers of the damned. Lucifer, the fallen angel, stood on a throne made of obsidian and bone at the zircon, center of this phantom realm. His presence emanated chilling power, and his eyes were like flaming embers.

Azrael, the Angel of Death, has stood on the edge of the heavens for ages. He had witnessed the birth and death of stars, the rise and fall of civilizations, and the never-ending cycle of existence. But his eyes lingered on the wicked seat like that of a raven. Azrael's rapacity was so enormous that he was unfazed by the absurdity of the vast intellectual depth and sinew of the Hellish throne, which was held by the fallen angel Lucifer for millennia.

Azrael was yearning for power. He craved the ability to exert influence over whispers and shadows and to become the supreme judge of life and death. The dark nectar of Hell's power was the only thing that could slake his hunger, which was a festering wound in his soul.

Unknown to himself, Azrael crossed the celestial boundary one starry night while wearing his darkness. He fell into the chasm, his wings ripping at the very fabric of existence as they brushed against it. He descended to the throne of Lucifer, his appearance a sharp contrast to the hall's otherworldly splendor.

"Lucifer, I have come for your throne," Azrael hissed in a scratching whisper.

With awareness of Azrael's approach, Lucifer exhaled a low, rumbling laugh that reverberated throughout Hell's corridors.

'*How about that?*' Lucifer ruminated. '*The Angel of Death, Azrael, is vying for control over the doomed.*' An iniquitous simper tarried at the sides of the Dark Prince's thin lips. He further ideated with the insolent idea and mused: '*An odd suggestion.*'

Lucifer continued to perpend, '*The Angel of Death would not have been the first to see a chimera in his imagination if there had been an inhumane integer in the cosmic vault of the preposterous terminus.*'

"Such nonsense, has He sent you? And to effectuate what capacity?"

"No one has sent me, I come on my own."

"Is that right, Azrael?" Lucifer's smile widened. "You have no will of your own."

"You have been plighted with the wheedling and the blandishment of the mortals, the pursuit of insuperable conquest, a derisory and a disparaging credence, a challenge for the fools."

Lucifer's long and handsome face became distorted, slanted with the memory of the day he was cast out. He tried to veil the scruple that his entire being beetled, distended to anyone who was watching the discourse. "How dare you?"

With a steely voice, Azrael declared, "Lucifer, I am not here to play games." "I intend to seize what is rightfully mine."

Rising from his nephrite throne, Lucifer's eyes blazed with a fierce rage that only Azrael could have dared to kindle. His demonic force was concealed by the grace with which he moved.

"And why do you believe it is legitimately yours?" With a trace of derision, his voice was a seductive whisper as Lucifer questioned. "You are merely death's messenger." I am the master of darkness, the king of the damned. I own this territory, and I will hold it until the stars go out.

Unaffected by Lucifer's disobedience, Azrael called upon the strength of the emptiness he had within. He unleashed a wave of pure, unadulterated death that enveloped the throne room, causing the walls of Hell to shudder.

Azrael, though, was unmoved. The attraction of total dominance and power overcame any hesitancy or fear. He was aware that the road to the throne would be perilous and full of obstacles that would severely test his willpower.

Azrael set to work methodically, creating his web of deceit. He made pacts with disobedient demons and enticed gullible people to support him. His might aggrandize with every victory, and the demon legions muttered his name in awe and fear.

As Azrael's power extended throughout the Domain of Darkness, Lucifer realized how dangerous he was. At first, the fallen angel observed with amusement, considering Azrael's goal to be a foolish endeavor. But Lucifer's laughter gave way to worry as Azrael's army became stronger.

It was inevitable that Azrael and Lucifer would face off in a cosmic struggle that would decide Hell's fate. Enormously strong and motivated by their unshakeable goals, the two angels readied themselves for a battle that would permanently upset the equilibrium of the infernal domain.

In the depths of the steatite heart of Hell, the stage was set for a war that would shake the very foundation of existence. Azrael, the Angel of Death, and Lucifer, the fallen angel, stood face to face, their eyes locked in a deadly gaze that promised annihilation.

A vast and frozen demesne where shadows swirled and darkness remained, the Devil, the Prince of Lies, cast a venomous stare at the Earth. His crimson eyes burned with envy as he saw Jesus, the Son of God, descend from the skies on the shoulders of two radiant angels. His long brown hair appeared to be wet with beads of water hanging at the edges to preach a message of love and redemption.

"Here comes trouble." The Dark Prince whispered under his breath, not amused at all. "But he comes for the Church and his bride." Lucifer consoled himself with the averring of end-time prophecies. Yet deep inside, the banished expatriate knew *why* he was witnessing the mise-en-scène of Biblical proportions and became ever more spectacular whenever he, the cursed one, turned to look from a safe distance.

Following his celestial descent, Jesus emerged from the ethereal nothingness, his body exhausted from the long voyage. Despite his physical infirmity, his spirit glowed with a steadfast drive to reignite the hearts of the faithful.

He set out, a lone figure striding among the crowd, his presence eliciting both amazement and terror. The scars from his fall remained evident, but they reminded all who witnessed and believed in his sacrifice and compassion.

As farcical and lunkheaded as the reasoning may be dissembled, the blarneying was inescapable for Lucifer's coaxing in the face of the polemic vitriol he was encountering and trying to digest as the young majestically resplendent prophet got closer to land, a substratum whose shape and form, along with the terminus of the Divine design had been polluted and contaminated, warped by men and women who the dark prince was successful in baiting and drawing in towards the eternal darkness, the zip code to our rebel without a cause; which, turns out, became the keynote, bedecked with lies and deception and the end to all morality and everything sacred.

This devil is some piece of work.

In the boiling depths of Hell, amidst the moans of the condemned and the stifling stench of brimstone and genocidal flesh burning (a people chosen but then denounced by God Himself when the transgressed, and kept at it until the term 'women and children' bore no consequence whatsoever – the Bani-Israel had proved time and again to be the bane of mankind; not Old boy Lucifer but the pernicious slaves of Egypt.

Lucifer, the Prince of Darkness, sat on his lapis-lazuli throne. His eyes, once filled with pride and ambition, now sparked with icy, burning terror.

For millennia, he ruled the underworld with an iron fist, commanding his demonic hordes. But suddenly, a tremor rippled across the depths, chilling him to the core. A dazzling glow descended from the heavens, throwing an ethereal radiance over the underworld.

As the celestial light neared, Lucifer's sharp senses felt a presence unlike any he had before met. It projected a sense of purity, benevolence, and unmistakable authority that sent chills down his spine. It was the presence of Jesus, the Son of Man.

A flood of horror washed over Lucifer. He realized that Jesus' arrival would herald the end of his reign. For generations, he had attempted to poison humanity, turning their hearts away from God and toward the abyss. But now his greatest adversary has arrived to undo all his evil acts.

With shaky hands, Lucifer rose from his throne and approached the brink of the terrible pit. As Jesus descended, his gaze met Lucifer's, causing the devil to experience extreme terror. In that moment, he saw the full force of the divine and the futility of his resistance.

"What? What is this?" Lucifer murmured, barely audible above a hiss.

"It is the end for you, Lucifer," Jesus said, his voice comforting (not to Satan) amid the tumult. "Your reign of terror has ended."

"My reign of terror?" He laughed nervously, "You say it as if I have the faculty to sanction deportment during the bitter, if not downright cruel home that your Father has made for these ungrateful creatures that cannot show self-restraint even with the threat of hell looming over their ugly heads."

"You were once a model of self-restraint and class, oh cursed one, what happened?"

"You know what happened and with Whose will." He smiled a sad smile. "The state of being is giving a hostage or a million to fate."

***

Mary of Bethany

Initially, doubt persisted. Many had witnessed his descent but were skeptical of his divinity. They questioned his motivations and his capacity to fulfill the prophecies. However, as Jesus began to cure the sick, calm storms, and perform miracles, a spark of faith appeared in the hearts of individuals.

One such person was Mary of Bethany, a woman who had given up hope following the death of her brother, Lazarus. When Jesus approached her and said, "I am the resurrection and the life," a deep faith burned within her. When Lazarus was revived, Mary's heart filled with thanks and faith.

The news of Jesus' miracles spread like wildfire, attracting followers from every walk of life. He lectured on love, forgiveness, and the kingdom of God, mesmerizing audiences with his wisdom and compassion. Individuals came forward one by one, their doubts and anxieties transformed by renewed faith.

Among these followers was Simon Peter, a modest fisherman whose life was changed by a meeting with Jesus. Despite his early reservations, Peter personally witnessed the power of God acting through him. He became a faithful apostle, preaching the message of salvation across the land.

***

The religious establishment's antagonism to Jesus rose in tandem with his reputation. They viewed him as a challenge to their authority and attempted to undermine his beliefs. Nonetheless, Jesus remained strong, and his persistent faith inspired his followers.

In the face of persecution and misfortune, the faithful held fast to their beliefs. They understood that Jesus had come to redeem them from their sins and give them eternal life. Their faith in him was unshakeable, and it was this unflinching faith that eventually prevailed.

Man, since the beginning of time, has tried to intercede with the Supreme Authority with his dragooned sense of divinity and the idols made of stone, which break, and then the man asks why God breaks.

Similar to the parable of Abraham when he destroyed a great number of man-made deities and left one standing. When the townsfolk returned and asked, and some pointed fingers at Abraham, he immediately repudiated those accusations, telling them to ask the one idol that he had left standing with the axe hanging on one stony, lifeless shoulder.

"Go ask her (Ceres), for I have nothing to tell."

"How can she tell?"

"I thought she was the divine embodiment of agriculture and the development of crops, particularly wheat." He looked around. No one said anything, but all of them were fuming at the ears.

"Didn't she oversee plowing into Tellus (the Roman Earth goddess) as well as sowing and the nurturing of seed?" Abrahan had spoken in a calm yet exacting tone, his voice a mixture of definitive certitude and regnant piousness; "And now your eyes tell me that she, a goddess of…" He had looked to his father, who stood among the tribesmen, his love for his son was slowly turning into disdain, and he looked on disparagingly.

Abraham had broken eye contact and resumed to address the seething mob of disbelievers and mischief makers and men suffering from malfeasance, foolhardiness, greed, lies, and conceit that would benefit them for only but a short time.

A young Abraham did not breach gait: "Goddess of whatsoever you feel bound by, is unable to strike a fly despite all that power?" He had smirked much to the onlookers' belligerence. "Such nonsense."

His hands moved quietly; his voice was clear and sonant; his words were few and polite, yet they struck the unbelievers and the mischief-makers with the ferocity of a spear.

What could the men do but build a fire like a fire had never been built before and hurtled the prophet of God with the help of a catapult – since no man could go even a few hundred feet close to the fire when the inferno flared at its supreme, something similar to Nebuchadnezzar and the 'four men' of Babylon; Shadrach, Meshach, and Abednego and a mysterious stranger.

Nevertheless, despite his physical weakness, Jesus triumphed in his quest to garner trust and faith from the faithful. His miracles, teachings, and sacrifice ignited a flame of belief that would burn brightly for generations to come, transforming the hearts and minds of countless individuals and forever shaping the course of human history.

***

From his residence in the depths of Hell, the Devil had become more concerned about Jesus' rising impact on humanity, similar to how he had become at the time of Abraham. He witnessed how people came to the savior's lectures, eager to hear his message of hope and salvation. This constituted a significant threat to the Devil's control over mortal hearts and thoughts.

Determined to impede Jesus' purpose, the Devil took on the shape of a terrifying monstrous creature, his jagged teeth bared and his claws dripping with poison. He appeared to Jesus in the barren wilderness, where the Son of God had fasted for forty days and nights.

The Deception Before the Battle

Despair swept over Lucifer as he saw the full scope of his foolishness. He knew if he were to battle against this tall and lean man of God, he would lose. His pride and ambition would fall to dust before the brilliant majesty of Jesus.

As Jesus continued his empyreal descent, the darkness of Hell dissipated, replaced by a warm and comfortable light. Lucifer stared in dismay as his demons, who had formerly been loyal followers, failed and turned to ashes. The infernal world, long a bastion of evil, was being purified and redeemed.

And suddenly, as Jesus' brilliant form reached the depths of Hell, there was a terrible hush. The wailing of the doomed stopped, and the stink of brimstone faded. In its place, a beautiful silence reigned, a tranquility that had been missing for many centuries.

They both found themselves in the middle of some kind of a vast space of land with only sand and wind, perhaps a desert.

The wind whipped at Jesus's threadbare robes, whistling a mournful tune. His stomach churned a hollow ache echoing the emptiness of the vast, unforgiving landscape. Forty days and nights, he'd been here, wrestling with his mortality, his body a vessel for the divine yet fragile and weary. He'd been tested, tempted, and pushed to the very edge of his strength.

And now, a new test.

A small figure stumbled into his field of vision, a girl no more than six, her clothes tattered, her face smudged with dust. Her eyes, a shocking blue, met his with a desperate plea.

"Please, sir," she whimpered, her voice barely a whisper. "I'm lost. Can you help me?"

Jesus felt a pang of sympathy. He knelt before her, his heart aching for the lost and the vulnerable. 'Of course, little one. What is your name?'

"Lily," she mumbled, her gaze dropping to the sand.

Her desperation tugged at him, a familiar ache and the echo of his humanity. He reached out, his fingers brushing against the rough fabric of her dress.

"Where is your home, Lily?"

"I… I don't know," she said, her voice trembling. "I was with my father, but he's gone. I'm lost, all alone."

A deep, almost instinctive fear stirred within him. He saw a flicker of something in her eyes, something he couldn't quite name. A cunning intelligence, a manipulative light.

"Don't worry, Lily," he whispered, his voice gentle. "We will find your father. I will help you."

He rose, picking her up. The warmth of her tiny frame against his chest was a stark contrast to the chilling wind. He began to walk, his gaze scanning the dunes, searching for any sign of a lost soul.

But as they walked, a strange sensation crept over him. The girl's weight felt heavier than it should. Her grip on his neck tightened, and his breath grew shallow. As he tried to speak, his voice croaked as if the desert had become his throat.

"Lily," he whispered, his voice weak. "Are you… alright?"

She chuckled, a sound that echoed with a chilling familiarity. "Of course, dear Jesus. Why would you think I wouldn't be?"

Her eyes, once a plea for help, now gleamed with a malevolent glow. There was no innocent child in them, only the cunning glint of a seasoned adversary.

"You are so naive," she hissed, her voice now a serpent's hiss. "You know, I can give you everything you desire. Power, glory, dominion over all creation. All you have to do is… relinquish your path."

The truth dawned on Jesus, chilling him to the bone. This wasn't a lost child. This was Lucifer, disguised in the guise of innocence, coming to tempt him one final time.

With a shuddering breath, Jesus tightened his grip. He held Lily close, his heart pounding against her deceptively fragile frame.

"The path I walk is not dictated by desire, Lucifer," he said, his voice raspy with the exertion of his spirit. "It's dictated by love. And love does not demand, it gives."

He pressed his lips against Lily's forehead, a silent prayer for her soul to be saved. He felt a rush of power, a fierce light emanating from within him. The desert around them shimmered, the wind howling in a cacophony of raw energy.

Lily shrieked, her true form flickering beneath the surface of the innocent child. He saw a whirlwind of darkness, a monstrous shadow reaching out to devour him. But his faith, his love, was a beacon, a fire that burned brighter than the shadows.

He felt her slip from his grasp, a phantom figure dissolving back into the desert sand. The wind fell still, and the desert was quiet.

Alone again, with the sun rising over the horizon, Jesus felt the weight of his struggle, the victory of his unwavering faith. But the battle was far from over. He knew, with a certainty that chilled him, that Lucifer would return. The desert was vast, and the temptations of power were as enduring as the human heart.

He continued his journey, his gaze fixed on the horizon, a silent prayer for his soul and the souls of others lost in the vastness of the world.

Back in the desert, his form now withered and his spirit broken, Lucifer collapsed upon the ground. His evil empire had been shattered, and his reign as the Prince of Darkness had ended. Yet he wanted to take Jesus on, mano-a-mano.

The air crackled with the residue of power, and the aroma of sulfur hung in the air like desperation. Lucifer, once brilliant in his basalt armor, lay battered and broken, a true fallen angel. He stared up at Jesus, the conqueror, with eyes full of incredulity and grudging adoration.

Lucifer's voice was scratchy as he said, "You...you bested me." He reached for his blade, but it was swallowed up in the whirling miasma of defeat.

Jesus was dressed in an all-black large shawl (mantle), which had tassels; a distinctively Jewish tallith in a form it was in antiquity. Black linen stood over him, a silent presence emitting an almost intolerable light. He gave Lucifer a hand, his eyes brimming with compassion.

The dark prince was taken aback, yet he kept saying when he should've stopped 6047 years ago.

"You may have defeated me..."

Jesus was quick to restrict and voice in the most calming voice that the dark lord had ever heard, "You are not defeated, Lucifer," Jesus stated calmly. "You are simply lost."

Lucifer snorted, producing an unpleasant rasp. "Lost? Is the Morning Star, the bringer of light, lost? You speak to me about loss while wielding the might of the cosmos itself?"

Jesus didn't flinch. "Power does not define you, Lucifer. Your path is determined by your choice and will."

"Choice?" Lucifer laughed with a hollow tone. "I am tied by fate, by the very threads of destiny. I am the serpent, the shadow, and the perpetual opponent. I am the contradiction that gives your light meaning."

"A meaning you have chosen, Lucifer," Jesus said. "You accepted the darkness, even when it threatened to engulf you. You've struggled against the light not because you hate it but because you're afraid of it. You fear the reality it reveals: that you, too, are capable of love, hope, and salvation. You disobeyed and contested then protested then oppugned Sovereignty itself, willing to brazen hellfire at the end of it all."

"The end appeared to be very far away."

"Yet you knew there was an end, and hence you asked Him for respite until 'the day.' I feel sorry for you, Azazel, even when your singular purpose is to mislead His creation from a path He made for them to tread."

Lucifer remained motionless, his gaze fixated on the distant horizon, where the sun was about to rise. He saw the light, a brilliant, ethereal radiance that ridiculed his gloom.

"You offer me atonement," Lucifer replied, his voice straining. "How can I be redeemed if I am permanently shackled to the shadows?"

"You are not chained," Jesus continued, his voice forceful yet gentle. "You are free to choose. You are free to go out of the darkness and into the light. It is a decision you must make for yourself."

"Really?" Lucifer tried to mock Jesus, but it didn't work.

Jesus knelt beside Lucifer; his gaze steadfast. "Yes, my dear, *really*. Azazel, you are not your darkness. You are a spirit lost in the maze of your creation. You can find your way out and back home."

Lucifer stared at the offered hand, a silent battle raging within him. He saw the light reflected in Jesus' eyes, a light that mirrored his own, a light he had buried deep within. He felt a flicker of hope, the faintest whisper of a truth he had long suppressed.

Slowly, hesitantly, Lucifer placed his hand in Jesus'. The touch sparked a jolt of light, scorching his skin. But it was not an unpleasant pain. Instead, it was the sting of a healing wound, a promise of something new.

"Perhaps," Lucifer whispered, his voice barely audible. "Perhaps I am not so lost after all."

Jesus knew that the fallen angel in front of him could never be trusted. "Do you truly believe that, or will you strike at me from behind?" There was a silence that lasted an eternity before Jesus spoke again. "I have come not to judge the world but to rescue it."

Lucifer's lips parted slightly in a crestfallen yet perverse and rigid grin. "You believe you can save these wretched souls?" The Devil snarled, his voice like a snake's whisper. "You are only a pawn in your Father's hands, a tool for enslaving others."

Jesus faced the Devil's gaze with steadfast resolve. Despite his physical frailty from the extended travel, his spirit was filled with the fire of his goal. "Don't call Him father."

The devil ignored Jesus and went on. "Father sanctioned…"

"Do not call Him father!" Jesus yelled this time, "He begets not, nor is He begotten." Big J continued: "For God so loved the world that he is willing to send his best men to bring the lost sheep

back to the road that leads to heaven, only for you to whisper misgivings into their ears.”

The Devil chuckled mockingly. “I have no power over them but the capacity to mislead and influence. What your men do is listen to me and abandon God, despite knowing that they are being lied to or that the fulfillment of desire is only but a fleeting moment in the vast illusion of time, which may or may not be.” He looked at Jesus. “I bear no responsibility, but I accept my fate, unlike you, young man.”

As Jesus was about to say something, Lucifer barged in with even more filial piety: “Is there eternal life? There is no such thing. Death awaits us all, and your precious God cannot stop it.”

“I am the resurrection and the life,” Jesus answered. “Whoever believes in my Father and his vicegerents on Earth, though he dies, will live.”

“Even he who comes after you.”

“Let’s not pull him into this, Azazel. This time, you and I talk. Your time will come if you survive this.”

“He will come if I survive this.”

“He will come only when I go, but he will come.”

A furious struggle of wills erupted, with the Devil enticing Jesus with promises of power and glory. But Jesus stayed steady in his faith, refusing the Devil's every temptation.

"Get behind me, Satan," Jesus said. "For it is written, you shall worship the Lord, your God, and him only shall you serve.'"

***

The Battle

In the relentless expanse of a barren desert, where the scorching sun hung high, and the sand danced in ephemeral swirls, a celestial clash of titans unfolded. Jesus stood resolute, his radiant gaze piercing the oppressive heat. Opposing him, Lucifer, the fallen angel, his once-angelic countenance twisted into a mask of malevolence.

As the ground beneath them trembled, the two adversaries unleashed their celestial might. Jesus raised his hands, and a blinding light enveloped him, casting ethereal shadows across the dunes. From his lips poured forth words of compassion and forgiveness, a symphony of grace that reverberated through the desolate landscape.

Lucifer, in his defiance, conjured a maelstrom of darkness. Inky tendrils lashed out like venomous serpents, seeking to ensnare

Jesus' soul. But the Son of God remained unyielding, his love an impenetrable barrier against Lucifer's sinister allure.

With each passing moment, the battle raged with ferocity. Jesus' miracles flickered through the darkness, healing the wounded Earth and raising withered palms to life. Lucifer's temptations whispered through the sand, promising power and dominion.

As the sun began its descent, casting an eerie orange glow upon the scene, the decisive moment arrived. Jesus raised the cross, a symbol of his ultimate sacrifice, and charged at Lucifer. The fallen angel roared in defiance, but his darkness could not withstand the overwhelming power of love.

With a thunderous crash, Lucifer's form dissolved into nothingness, his hateful presence banished from the holy ground. The desert exhaled a collective sigh of relief as the celestial battle ended.

In the aftermath of the cataclysm, Jesus stood victorious, his wounds a testament to his enduring compassion. The dunes had become a symbol of hope, where darkness had been overcome by the radiant light of God's love. And as the stars twinkled above, the desert whispered tales of the epic battle that had forever etched itself into its eternal sands.

***

The Devil was defeated and fled to the depths of Hell. His attempt to stop Jesus had failed. The Son of God had proven himself too powerful, and his purpose was too divine.

From that day onward, Jesus continued his travels, sharing his message of love and redemption with anyone who would listen. Even though the Devil continued to try and torment him, Jesus triumphed, his faith unwavering and his mission unchanging.

As the sun rose and painted the sky in gold and scarlet, Lucifer and Jesus stood side by side, two beings bathed in the same light, two souls faced with the same decision: darkness or redemption. The future remained uncertain, but at that moment, among the rubble of a struggle fought and won, a ray of hope appeared. There was still time for Lucifer, the fallen angel, to rise again, not as the bringer of darkness but as the keeper of light, demonstrating the power of choice and the enduring promise of redemption.

***

Chapter 7: Finding His Power

Lucifer's Final Decision

Jesus the prophet of God stood in the vastness of the celestial kingdoms, where ethereal light flowed like liquid gold. He exuded warmth and was a lighthouse of compassion and optimism. But behind all of this heavenly splendor, there was still a shadow, an apparition that had danced in the light of heaven but was now trapped in the maze-like depths of hell. It was the fallen angel Lucifer, imprisoned in a prison he had built for himself.

Lucifer has struggled with the agony of his decisions for ages. His descent from grace reverberated through the endless halls of the afterlife like a woeful ballad. The brilliant fires of revolt flickered alive in his heart, reminding him of his former glory. His immortal essence, the remnants of his eternal spirit, was mocked by the darkness that enveloped him now, clinging to him like a mist.

Lucifer sat beside a dark river, alone in the abyss, its waters echoing the turmoil of a thousand lost souls. Their shouts resonated like a discordant choir off the obsidian walls of hell as they whirled about in agony. Occasionally, their hopelessness crept into him, reminding him of the power he had as the tempter, and for a brief instant, he experienced life once again. But when the weight of their suffering consumed him, the excitement quickly gave way to despair.

"O Tempter, why do they suffer?" A voice rose over the darkness, from somewhere close by. The figure, still flickering with the last of the light, was that of a soul. "You used to be their leader. Why not save them from this shadow of death?"

With turmoil in his gaze, Lucifer raised his head. "Because I am lost," he retorted. "I have become what I once resisted. I once sought to elevate the souls of humankind, but now I revel in their madness. They have become my art, a twisted masterpiece, and I am nothing but a relic of my former self."

The voice begged, shaking with the weight of hope, "Then rise again. Teach them the value of making a decision. You can illuminate the path."

The words ignited the embers of redemption that were still buried beneath the layers of despair, penetrating Lucifer's dark heart. As he stood, he felt the chains of his creation binding him to darkness. He was torn, teetering on the edge of the abyss and the salvation that beckoned from above.

Above him, an ethereal doorway suddenly opened, letting down the brilliant light of heaven like a starry cascade. Bathed in celestial brilliance, a familiar shape appeared – that of Jesus, the prophet, the personification of forgiveness and love. His stare was demanding yet kind at the same time as it was penetrating.

"Our paths cross once again, oh Lucifer." Jesus smiled.

"Not you, again."

"Lucifer," Jesus spoke, his voice a balm to the tortured soul. "The choice has always been yours. You were not created to be the keeper of darkness but the bearer of light. Your fall does not define you. It is your choices, in this moment, that will shape your destiny."

Lucifer hung his head, the weight of his actions unfurling around him like shadows retreating in the light. "But how can I redeem myself, when the very nature of my existence draws me back to the darkness? What if there is no way out?"

"You can't have it your way all the time."

"Perhaps," Lucifer looked to the ground, avoiding eye contact, "However, Je... whatever your name is, my heirloom refuses to regard that." He looked up again and just like the first time, a wave of terror swept throughout Lucifer. "Leave me alone, oh prophet of God."

"I cannot do that."

"Then join me."

"In what? The pursuit of self-despair? The grand betrayal on a pittance through your slough of despondency?

Lucifer simply kept looking at Jesus, as hard it was, the fallen angel was, after all, an unyielding, intransigent creature of God.

"Redemption is not a path absent of difficulty," Jesus continued, stepping closer, his presence radiant with love. "It is a journey of choice, a battle against your fears. The power of choice lies within you, Lucifer. You can inspire hope instead of despair. You can be a keeper of light."

Lucifer eyed Jesus until he couldn't. With every word of Jesus, the miasma of his torment began to intensify. Memories of his celestial existence flooded back – the laughter of the seraphim, the joy of creation, and the love of the Father. All lost to insolence!

He remembered what it felt like to soar among the stars, unfettered by the chains of bitterness and rage. He felt the rumination would cause his head to fulminate with dark forebodings of his detrimental, grievous deviltry. He lowered his head again and whispered something inaudible.

"I heard that."

"Did you, now?"

"I have ruined your preponderant debased, ungodly dominance before. I will not hesitate to do so again; and now you are weaker than before, be mindful of the trouncing, you have foundered far from your debauched réclame. I thought…"

"That is all irrelevant, meaninglessly; you will see, oh prophet of God, you will witness my morning jolt." With that Lucifer tried to flee with his hands covering his ears, to get as far away from Jesus as he possibly could. Unfortunately, he did not hear what Big J had to say in the end.

However, the temptation loomed, alluring and dark, soughing promises of grandeur through mayhem. The specters of his fallen nature gnawed at him, seeking to drag him back into the shadows, and his heart raced.

"What if your heart falters again?" Jesus queried. "I know you can hear me, Lucifer."

"Then I shall rise and choose again," Lucifer promised, the light around him intensifying. "The struggle does not diminish my worth, nor does it limit my capacity for divine antipathy."

"Believe in the infinite possibilities of redemption, Lucifer."

"Oh, shut up, *you beatnik flower child*!" He scorned, his tone replete with derision and ridicule.

A bemused Jesus shook his head. "Why don't you accept it?"

"Accept what? Why are you smiling?"

"That you seek redemption yet, once again, your vainglory blinds you. I smile because you don't."

"Vainglory… Ha. What's next, pompous audacity?"

"Don't make it even more tangled. Have faith in the countless opportunities for reconciliation, Lucifer." Jesus repeated himself.

It became clear to him what to do in an instant. Lucifer's fingers trembled in the air as he stretched out, grabbing for the light that promised transformation, his pulse racing with terror and eagerness. The blackness shuddered as he did, recoiling, threatening to engulf him. He pulled his hand back, *'What was I thinking?'*

With a radiant burst, the chains around his heart tautened and clamped, and he descended through the portal, hosted by snake-like ropes of humiliation, and ignominy. As he floated into the realm of sublunary, the shadows of his past still danced around his feet, they held immense power over him. He was further defined by his fall.

Through his decrepit, hoary dismal blackness, Lucifer began to see the suffering souls still trapped in darkness. With neglect thriving within him, he turned to them.

"I am here," he declared, the might of his voice echoing through the netherworld. "And I will guide you towards the dark."

In that moment, he became, once again, the harbinger of chaos.

The keeper of hope simply looked at him with his deep brown eyes – a reminder that even in the darkest corners of existence, the power of choice and the perjury of castigation could misrepresent the way home. "May you be saved, *Iblees*, lost child of His."

***

The wails of the doomed and the sharp stench of sulfur filled the air in Hell. With his pride crushed and his wings burnt, Lucifer prowled the barren terrain, a shell of the stalwart 'Morning Star' he once was. The exact person he had previously ridiculed – Jesus Christ – had vanquished him and thrown him back into the chasm. However, Lucifer was not to be broken. He was the King of Hell, the Devil, and he was going to rise again.

He reminisced about the magnificent times when he was God's right-hand angel/demon hybrid and the finest angel/demon hybrid. Then came the uprising, the collapse, and the crushing weight of failure. He had created a world of never-ending suffering, but it seemed to be a collapsing monument to his own conceit. To reign, he required more than just a wasteland.

His stare penetrating the limitless darkness, he stalked the depths in a sinister and menacing demeanor. He came upon devils, their souls twisted and broken, each more hideous and hopeless than the last. He addressed them like a fellow exile rather than their superior, master. He apportioned, almost reciprocated his vision, a revelation of a Hell not merely based on torment, but on order, on power, on a new kind of dominion.

His investigation took him to a tunnel of whirling turmoil concealed deep within Hell. This was the core of Hell's suffering and the origin of its strength. A primitive force, that connected with Lucifer's fallen nature, tugged at him. When he put his palm into the whirling chasm, he felt a sudden rush of energy. It was power, it was comprehension, and it was suffering. He was able to sense the very fabric of Hell, the unadulterated chaos that gave it form.

Nights became days, and days became years. Experimenting, Lucifer tested the limits of his newly acquired dominance over the chaos pools. He gained the ability to control their chaotic energy, bending, twisting, and sculpting it to suit his needs. He crafted landscapes of torment, forged rivers of fire, and conjured monstrous creatures to guard his dominion. Each success brought a surge of power, a sense of triumph that fueled his ambition.

He built a throne of obsidian and bone, a testament to his mastery over the infernal realm. He summoned the demons, those who had once been broken and tormented, and made them his agents. They were no longer slaves to Hell, but his subjects, their fear replaced by a twisted loyalty.

The screams of the damned resonated through the halls of Hell, but now they were a symphony of power, a testament to Lucifer's reign. He had transformed Hell, not into a place of pure torment, but into a reflection of his fallen majesty. His victory was not over God but over the chaos itself. He was no longer the fallen angel, but the King of the Underworld, a dark and terrible ruler who commanded the very essence of Hell.

And Lucifer realized that the voyage was far from being accomplished as he gazed at his realm. Though he had conquered Hell, he harbored fresh ambitions. He had no intention of halting until he completely altered the world until all creation bent before his will. His fall was merely a prelude, the beginning of his ascent to true power. His reign had just begun.

***

Vindicate all Lament

The acrid redolence of despair and brimstone permeated the sweltering biosphere and clung to Lucifer's flesh like a lifelong memento of his downfall and the crushing force of his disobedience. He paced the confines of his throne room, a vast cavern of blackened gemstones, its emptiness glassed the hollowness within him.

The fire that once burned in his soul, the fire of ambition and defiance, had dwindled to a flickering ember. Eternity weighed him down with an intolerable burden of sorrow and shame. He had battled for a world that had turned into a mockery of his ideals, and he had waged war against Heaven. He was now doomed to reign in a kingdom of pain, a warped mirror to his broken soul.

His demons, his loyal cohorts, watched him with a mixture of fear and pity. They saw the flicker of doubt in his eyes, the tremor in his hand that he struggled to suppress. They knew their lord was not the invincible tyrant they had once believed him to be. He was broken, a king in ruins.

The echoes of his defeat still resonated within him. Every whisper of torment, every cry of despair, was a tangible reminder of his failure. He had failed to create a world of freedom, a world of equality. He had instead forged a kingdom of pain, a prison built on the foundation of his own shattered dreams.

His mind was a chaotic battlefield. The echoes of his former glory clashed with the whispers of doubt. Images of his past victories mingled with visions of his downfall. He saw the faces of the angels he had once called brothers, their eyes filled with pity and condemnation. He saw the faces of his fallen comrades, their souls consumed by eternal torment.

He yearned for the touch of Heaven, for the warmth of the Father's embrace. But he knew it was a yearning that could never be fulfilled. He was forever bound to this realm, to this suffocating darkness. He was the architect of this incubus, and he had no one to blame but himself.

The weight of his solitude was grievously unendurable. He yearned for companionship, for understanding, for a single soul that would look past his fallen status and see the force he once was. He hankered for redemption, but then his pride would fog his reasoning, every single time.

In the darkest depths of Hell, malaise burned with rage within him. A desperate affliction, a spiritual apathetic discharge of bodily fluids, that perhaps, in the vast expanse of eternity, he could find a way to redress his coercers. A way to find peace in pristine pandemonium, not just for himself, but for the souls trapped within his dominion.

He closed his eyes, and images of his fallen comrades flashed through his mind. He saw their suffering, their pain, their endless agony. And he knew, with a certainty that pierced through the fog of his despair, that he must do something. He must find a way to consume their bane to make himself even more infernal, and reprehensible to make this kingdom, this realm of suffering, a lot more agonizing than any wretched human could have ever imagined. Even if it were a prophet like Jesus.

Even in the darkness, Lucifer found a drop of squalid purpose. He may be the King of Hell, but he was also the king of his destiny. And within that appliqué, fashioned with gossamers of guilt, regret, and despair, there was still room for a single thread of angst. He would find a way to redeem himself, not for the sake of Heaven, but for the sake of the souls in the Gehenna he had created. His muddled mind, a battlefield of internal conflicts, found a glimmer of solace in this single, unwavering, inverted resolve. But resolve nonetheless.

****

Chapter 8: Hell Unites

The Ashes of Retribution

"I watched with glee while your kings and queens – Fought for ten decades for the gods they made"[13]

The echoes of sadness thrummed with a tangible urgency in the twisted realms of the Kingdom of Hell, where shadows flicker like dying embers and a pallid hue radiates from the pools of molten anguish. The screams of haunted spirits rippled through the barren landscape, an orchestration that revealed secrets of anguish and despair, their agony serving as a constant reminder of the anarchy that prevailed. Under a sky tinged with red and black, the Devil arose from the ashes of his defeat, the pain of loss still fresh in his heart, but the need for retribution boiled inside of him.

The Devil rose from the ashes of his defeat in the depths of this dismal realm, the anguish of his failure still raw within him. He towered above the immediate shadows, which resembled the murmurs of the doomed. His eyes, which had once been glowing with accomplishment, had become dulled by unsettling sentiments, but something within him ignited a flicker of vengeance that was ready to devour all in its path.

---

[13] Songwriters: Keith Richards / Mick Jagger – Sympathy For The Devil lyrics © Abkco Music Inc.

"It's time," he slurred, his deliberate growl resonating through the oil-slick landscape. At his word, the ground shook, and the army of fallen angels moved, their wings a patchwork of tattered membranes blemished with the resentment of betrayal. Baal, Allocen, Baphomet, Behemoth, and Astoroth were among them; they were the specters of a great past that had been diminished to shadows of retribution.

With a voice full of honeyed malice, Baphomet murmured, "We have endured." He continued, "But we have festered under the weight of our damnation for far too long. The worlds above mock us for our pain. They think they can contain the whirlwind that we are. Are we going to be stuck in this horrible abyss forever?"

The Devil felt a familiar heat flare inside him as he listened carefully to his brethren's words of revenge. Their goal was to seize back control, to shatter the fragile calm above them, and to bring anarchy to the world of humans. Torn by suffering, though, his heart ached for more than just payback.

He clarified, "You misunderstand," with a thunderclap of his voice that silenced the assembly. "We are not only seeking retribution. Each cry from the depths serves as a reminder that they abandoned us. They think we are past the point of rising. We will demonstrate to them that we have emerged stronger, fiercer, and more prepared to take back what is truly ours after losing everything."

The others' eyes sparkled with a tenebrous desire as the Devil spoke. Hell breathed around them, simmering fires of grief waiting for something to ignite. The Devil waved his hand and conjured up a black vortex in front of them, symbolizing the raw energy they were about to spew on the world above.

"Through this passage, we will weave our way into the hearts of men," he vowed. "We're going to bring back hopelessness and engulf them in their misery. They will shudder and they will know our names."

The deity Allocer, The Great Duke of Hell, emerged from the shadows, a once-majestic figure diminished by the endless scorn of their fallen status. His eyes glowed faintly, a frail reflection of the majesty they once held., moved forward and spoke in a reverential voice, "My lord, lead us. Let us tear through the veil that separates our worlds and show them the folly of their defiance."

The Devil traversed the jagged ravines where ignorance and despair met, searching for Baal, the fierce demon of power and war. As he approached, the stench of sulfur and blood intensified, unveiling Baal's lair – a dread fortress of twisted metal and bone. The very ground throbbed beneath the foot, pulsating with echoes of lost glory.

The Embryos of Guerdon

"**I** am here, Baal," the Devil declared, his voice a chilling wind. "I call upon you to rise and regain your might. Together, we shall build a kingdom worthy of our legacy."

Emerging from the dark threshold, Baal's figure loomed large, his eyes glowing like dying stars. "Have you found your resolve? Hope flickers like a candle in the wind." He said in a voice that belonged to 111 men and women, the sound it made was of a church organ but with all notes inversed when the voices all spoke at once.

"I have," the Devil replied, an unyielding fire ignited within him. "Join me, and we shall ignite Hell into a realm of fear and respect!"

As Baal swore his allegiance, they set off with the others. Abaddon, known for his skill in circumventing the minds of both mortals and immortals, was discovered hiding in the nethermost pit of despair. As the Devil conjured a vision of grandeur before him, Abaddon's laughter rang out, dark and melodic.

"You wish to build a kingdom from chaos? Intriguing," he mused. "A dance of manipulation and malice awaits."

Together, they pressed on to claim Behemoth, the embodiment of brutish strength and insatiable hunger, coiling within gloomy caverns. "To rule Hell and flesh, you first must stake your claim in the oblivion above," Behemoth growled as he joined their ranks, his loyalty cemented with a promise of carnage.

Lastly, Astoroth, the harbinger of war, awaited their call in an eerie expanse of severed arms and dismembered dreams. With flattering words spun like silk, the Devil lured Astoroth from his misery. "Together, we will unravel the heavens and laugh as we watch the orb burn."

As his generals gathered, the air began to lose its acrid stench; an excitement thrummed within the atmosphere, resonating across the burning landscape. The collective power of the fallen angels surged as they united under the Devil's banner, their rebellions finally finding purpose—to reshape Hell into a formidable kingdom plotted for conquest.

As plans were laid bare in the shadows, whispers of dominion sparked fevered anticipation. The soul collection efforts were enhanced, the anguished cries turning into hymns of despair that served their dark ambitions. Souls, once seen as mere footnotes of agony, became instruments of power, fueling the echoes of their forthcoming ascendancy.

Yet, within their hearts pulsed an unending hunger—for vengeance against the heavens that had forsaken them. They trained in meticulously organized divisions, enemies no longer, but soldiers preparing for a war that spanned realms.

On one chilling night, as the moonlit shadows painted a morose ambiance, the Devil stood upon the obsidian throne, his gaze steady on the desolate horizon stretched before him. A tempest brewed; it whispered promises of an uprising unseen by the forces of good.

"My generals," he intoned, power vibrating with every syllable, "the time draws near to confront our former kin. We shall not be forgotten or caged in oblivion. Together, we will carve our legacy in the sky and rain terror upon the heavens!"

As their roars of defiance echoed through the desolate Kingdom of Hell, the air crackled with anticipation. The forces of chaos gathered beneath the banners of the fallen, and shadows of vengeance fused into one.

The Devil smiled a smile forged from fire and fury, as he watched his generals rally together. The Kingdom of Hell was ready to rise from its ashes; a night filled with whispers of rebellion unfurled before them, the darkest chapter of their ancient myth only just beginning.

Ever the strategist, Astoroth scowled, weighing the enormity of what they had to do. "But what of the seals? The defenders of the realm above won't simply stand idle. With their meager light, they will fight back. Divided, we have no chance, we need to be devious. We can penetrate their ranks together."

Shaking off the dust of despair, Behemoth growled in his low timbre, "Fret not, Astoroth. We are the storms that ravage the skies. Against our wrath, their guardians are but embers. But if we're going to take action, we have to act together. Let the pursuit of revenge be our anthem."

The decision was made. The fallen gathered, their will melding with the very nature of Hell, an overwhelming force that broke through the layers of reality. With eons of misery fueling his tidal wave of malevolence, the Devil led the charge, a tidal wave of malevolence fueled by centuries of suffering, a redoubt against the sky above where sweet light dangled like an unsuspecting meal.

And so, they surged forth, a torrent of blackness pouring into the world of humans, and everyone who ventured to look down into the chasm could sense their presence. Every pulse in their new home echoed with the fear they instilled; each soul stirred by an instinctual recognition of doom.

They whispered through the ears of mortals, igniting greed and lust within hearts once pure; they danced like specters in the night, leading innocents astray into the depths of temptation. War ravaged family ties, friendships evaporated, and the bonds forged by love crumbled under the weight of despair.

But soon enough, the guardians reared their luminous heads; a shimmering alliance of hope and virtue. They rallied against the unrelenting tide of darkness, wielding songs of prayer and shields of light. The echoes of despondency that had enveloped Hell morphed into an orchestra of mourning, crashing into the very essence of goodness.

It was then that the Devil realized the futility of his rage. For every soul they claimed, another was saved by the resolve of the virtuous. Despite wrath, they staggered against the tempest of despair; for while darkness may corrode, it cannot extinguish the fire of hope.

In that crucible of conflict, the moment crystallized, a shattering epiphany cleaved the air.

He questioned, his eyes glinting with knowledge like a dagger that hesitates to murder, "Is vengeance truly the answer?" He eyed his acolytes, "I didn't want to drown in a sea of futility; I wanted to reclaim our crown.

"Surely we ought to embrace this weight and this suffering." The devil concluded.

The blazing heavens at that moment echoed his uncertainty: '*Moooamy, Daaady*'

The contorted gloom became aware, glowing softly with awareness. The Devil directed his attention to the recesses of his own heart, the humanity he had previously abandoned in his alluring quest for power.

This struggle he now fought within was a most unusual thing. While the magnitude of choice was making Hell tremble, salvation was whispering its name into the darkness. Could grief lead to happiness? Is it possible to select an enlightened path while accepting the darkness?

The response gave rise to a glimmer of belief amidst a sea of misery, ready to cast a shadow over the entire world.

As the echoes of battle raged, both within and without, the Devil knew the time had come to reshape his fate. Whether he returned to the desolation after the fight or broke free of the chains of his past was yet unwritten, but one truth ignited a chorus deep in the Kingdom of Hell: even in the bleakest of realms, new beginnings could unfurl from the ashes of darkness.

And therein lay his greatest act of defiance, a choice, resonating audibly without malice, to embrace the light.

He surveyed his domain, those once-luminous halls now engulfed in darkness, a grim monument to his rebellion against the divine. As the Archangel of Darkness, he was cloaked in shadows, a figure of dread in this realm of desolation. His gaze fell upon the pools of despair; their bubbling surfaces murmured secrets of power that whispered his name. He stepped closer, feeling the bitter essence of collected souls ignite his very being. Yet, power alone wouldn't quell his restless spirit. A new fire burned within him; a fierce hunger for vengeance against the Almighty who cast him down to this wretched void.

*****

In the abysmal depths of the Kingdom of Hell, shadows intertwined with distress and hopelessness hung thick as smoke, the Devil stalked through his dominion, his form draped in tendrils of darkness, each step echoing with a mournful disharmony.

No longer adorned in the pristine hues of heavenly light, he was now crowned in the somber glory of the fallen, lost to the whispers of time and treachery. Once the Archangel of Light, he now embraced the mantle of the Archangel of Darkness. His kingdom was a regrettable monument to a celestial rebellion, which was a testament to his fall from grace.

The air crackled around him, laden with the weight of countless souls, eternally trapped in the torment of their making.

Groans of the disintegrated flickered at the edges of perception as if even in their dying moments, they sought the cessation of their suffering. Pools of despair bubbled in the dim light, swirling with the echoes of erased hopes and twisted dreams. Each pit exuded an essence that ignited the essence within him, feeding the flames of power that coursed through his being. But this power, vast as it was, lay barren against the gnawing hunger that had taken root in his heart; a thirst for vengeance against the Almighty, the god that wove the fabric of his misery.

"Agares!" he thundered, his voice rolling across the bare mournfulness like thunderclouds before an inevitable storm.

"Yes, my liege?" Agares, the demon of courage, replied, his voice draped in the weight of regret, echoing the despair that filled every crevice of Hell.

"Summon the Council of the Damned. We gather not merely for power. The time has come to retaliate against our Creator."

Agares inclined his head, with a quiet, almost imperceptible terror flickering in his eyes. The tension in the air thickened, coiling around them like a serpent, braced to strike.

As Agares hastened to rally their comrades, Allocen, the manipulator of illusion, and Behemoth, the grotesque embodiment of gluttony came forward the Devil's mind churned with fiery visions of insurrection. Great shadows overlapped in his thoughts, each forming an infernal medley, blending hues of fury and desperation.

Allocen, draped in wretched glamour, materialized next, her presence a fleeting flicker of what had once been. She twirled illusions of grandeur before him, visions of heaven, of the seraphim and their eternal repose, effulgent and blissful. Each image spurred something in the Devil, igniting the flames of envy that branded his core.

With a band of loyal souls now forming, their path led them to Beelzebub, the Lord of the Flies, who ruled with a blend of pestilence and cunning. In the chambers thick with rot, they found him overseeing a hive of twisted creatures, souls warped into unholy shapes. At their arrival, Beelzebub grinned, his eyes narrowing into slits.

"Building an empire, are we? A place of decay and dominance?" he questioned mockingly. But at the Devil's fiery retort, a spark kindled in Beelzebub's heart. He vowed to coat a montage of fear and despair across the lands above.

"Dearest master," Allocen purred, her voice dripping with venomous sweetness. "What is this vengeance you seek? Shall we not trade our chains for a kingdom anew?"

With his form morphing like a vapor, Beelzebub snarled, *"Hold your tongue, insect!"* He hissed, "It's well past time for abortive inquisitions. We must dictate the necessity of taking action. The outside world has witnessed our error, but they have not experienced our fury. Let's demonstrate to them our real might."

The Devil's eyes flared, and the air stilled. "A new kingdom?" Berith, one of the lost princes of hell and the demon of disobedience, gyrated through the darkened lair, the subverted prince understood the gravity of their plight. "What he seeks is more than an illusion, Allocen. It is real. It is revenge."

"Revenge?" Behemoth erupted, his voice a cacophony of madness and hunger, "What are we without the sustenance of our wrath? Nihilism is the fate of beasts!"

The Devil held up a hand, the night gathering around him and the shadows writhing violently, twisting and twirling. "My brethren, stop living in desperation by yourself. We are going to reawaken the hunger of the abandoned. We're going to rule supremely again!"

Astoroth hissed from behind a curtain of darkness, hovering in the shadows like the encroaching hopelessness of the unredeemed. "But God is watching out for us. His hand holds the souls of the damned like an iron grip. You want to overthrow the throne, but they are always on guard."

"Then we shall become unseen," the Devil hissed, a sinister smile curling upon his lips. "We shall seep into their dreams, whisper into their conscience, feeding their fears until they become nightmares. The Almighty cannot protect His people forever against the shadows that had once shone brightly from Him."

The fallen angels who had gathered felt the flames of allegiance revived, despite having been punished for millennia. Their emotions were once again bound by the ghosts of their mutual resentment as they looked at each other. Fear of Hell became a burning desire to oppose the divine light that had deceived them.

Days passed like gales of agony, and before long the fallen angels had forged their dark war, a whispered spell that wove itself into the fabric of the mortal world and ingrained terrifying visions in the minds of people. Gradually, the trust started to wane, uncertainty crept in like a quick poison, and the whispers became unholy roars.

With each passing day, fear morphed into despair, and despair turned to madness. The shadows grew heavier, with the entire mortal sphere teetering on the edge of ruin. As the Devil reveled in the chaos unleashed upon the Earth, a single thought gripped him: Would vengeance quench the insatiable hunger within him, or would it merely cast him further into an abyss of suffering?

***

"Our future depends not on what the gentiles will say, but on what the Jews will do!"[14]

As the seas of despair swelled and souls twisted endlessly in torment, the constant din of dismay birthed the echo of his inner turmoil, a reminder that every act of vengeance was but another chain forged around his being.

Yet amid his longing a flicker of doubt whispered and writhed in his core. Vengeance would bring him power, yes, but solace? Was it not a vanquished dream lost in the dark?

"I seek saintly annihilation," The Devil spoke to himself, a mantra of resolution. But there was a trembling in the depths of his voice, a trace of remorse that remained unwavering, like the final flicker of a divine light yearning for redemption.

The Devil stood at the brink of fate itself, staring into the terrifying chasm of his decisions, in the Kingdom of Hell, where screams were drowned out by darkness. He was a wretched, tormented rebel with a burning heart, bound forever in the bonds he had created.

---

[14] David Ben-Gurion: 1955 Independence Day Parade Speech

"No longer will I wallow alone in torment," he vowed, his voice echoing through the hollow corridors. "I will reclaim my dominion."

With the weight of his past dragging at his heels like an anchor, the Devil began his quest. He sought out the remnants of his once-mighty legions – the fallen angels who had stood by his side in the celestial war against Heaven. In the pits of Hell, bravados had become skeletal whispers, but their loyalty remained, festering like an unhealed wound.

***

Chapter 9: Warring Through the Ages

Prelude to a Sepulture – The Devil's Lament in Elysium's Folly

Within the pitiful depths of Hell, ensconced in a cloistered area of the cosmos where light never dared to shine, where the climate was thick with dismals and sulfur. It was an eruption of distorted forms and hues that defied earthly logic, fashioned by the essence of dread and despair. It was not the flaming furnace of old stories nor the abode of perpetual agony represented in humanity's folktales. Rather, it was a phantasmagoria.

The Devil was sitting by himself on a smoldering ash throne, his red eyes clouded up with sadness. With his fingers clenched into claws, he held a glass vial containing a liquid that swirled with luminescent colors.

The irony danced on his pallid lips; even the architect of sin sought solace.

The cursed one found himself in this bizarre mounting, not under the appraising eyes of acolytes or the fear of the damned, but suspended in an eternity of self-reflection caused by one unfortunate choice: the consumption of a hallucinogenic potion known to the spirits that passed through his domain as 'Elysium's Folly.' He was surrounded by flickering realities that were both jarring and oppressive, enveloping him in a web of hopelessness.

Every day felt like an eternity, each moment punctuated by the pandemonium of lost souls wailing for redemption.

"What have I done?" he mused, a thought surfacing through the murky depths of his mind. The memories of his comrades, Baal, Allocen, and the others, flitted before him like kelpies, flickering in the dim light.

Baal constantly planned to outperform others with his conceited hubris. He was ravenous for glory! Allocen cackled nonstop, spilling poison all over Hell, a poison that only sowed more strife. How could trust exist among such treachery as Beelzebub, the slothful wretch buried behind mountains of lies, and Behemoth, whose power was equaled only by his gluttony? In this world of shadows, friendship turned to treachery, devotion to one another into yearning, and he, the Devil, built his own confinement.

Who could he trust? None but the phosphorescent, dulcet sap. Distraught circumstances call for hysterical choking and knockbacks.

He brought the bottle to his lips and took a deep breath made painful by the sting of sulfur. The elixir ignited a paroxysm of desolate anguish behind his eyelids, sliding down his throat like an oily slick. For an instant, the weight of hopelessness lifted, and he was caught in a state of suspended animation, a moment of recollection blending with madness. Visions danced before him like autumn breezes full of leaves: gardens of paradise, heavenly laughter, bright faces, and the transient warmth of an embrace; things he'd unknowingly deserted.

The panorama changed abruptly, with demons whirling around like turbulent clouds and tearing at the sound of iron chains clanging. As the colors turned into dark shadows, fractals of power radiated in spirals, and he pondered, "Am I their master?"

He fell through layers of his existence. Every shade whispered mysteries of the cosmos and life beyond contempt to him. Had he given up contentment for power?

Did you exchange a walk on part in a war for a lead role in a cage?[15]

In the heart of this turmoil, deep sensations unfurled; the touch of moist grass, the innocent chirping of unseen birds. He saw himself soaring through valleys, untouched by evil.

"What is wrong with me?" The question pulsed within like a throbbing heartbeat, each beat echoing despair, taunting him.

Before him, a whirlwind of emerald flames flaunted the forms of Astoroth and Baal, their eyes shining with malevolent intent.

Baal mockingly said, "Look who's lost in his creation," reiterating what the Devil already knew. Flickering shadows turned into unfulfilled promises.

However, a calm, calm voice broke through the tumult.

"You are not defined by them," it cried out, resonating deep within him. "You are the architect of your own fate."

The clouds parted, revealing not just walls but windows, glimpses into realms where choice and consequence harmonized in peace.

A tidal wave of clarity washed over him. He never intended this desolation; he was the creator of realms, capable of benevolence. "Maybe, just maybe," he thought, "redemption lies not in despair but in understanding."

The potion flickered to a close, and Hell's jagged edges softened. The Devil, browbeaten and disillusioned, rose from his throne, not in fury but in resolution. For even he, the Prince of Darkness, could turn the tempest within into a journey toward full-blown retaliation. And thus, from that moment, began a new tale in the annals of eternity.

***

The Devil, who was formerly Lucifer, an archangel, had fallen from grace and lost his brilliant wings that had formerly allowed him to see the brightness of Heaven. Now, he clung to his shadows, surrounded by hideous greenery that caressed his ears like a lover's sorrow, whispering forgotten secrets in place of divine radiance. Everything was an ironic echo of God's previous acclaim for him, a taunting reminder of his fall.

As he drifted across the world, brilliant fractals danced before his eyes, exploding with vivid colors that painted fresh horrors across the black palette of his thoughts. It felt like falling into a pit, forever, a rich tartan tessellation of violet heavens and crimson earth saturated with writhing shadows.

The landscapes turned into clamors, appearing and disappearing like spectral phantoms, and oftentimes, they formed logical thoughts that threatened to drive him insane.

"Through all of history, mankind has ingested psychedelic substances. Those substances exist to put you in touch with spirits beyond yourself, with the creator, with the creative impulse of the planet."[16]

A whisper entered the room and struck at the center of him, asking, "Is this what you are reduced to?"

It was nasty and eerie, like the sound of laughter. "Shackled by your own designs, once loved by Heaven!"

Through the swirling mists of his hallucinogenic coma, the Devil beheld vague yet nevertheless recognized shapes. The hapless and twisted remnants of mankind, once drawn to them by their moral failings, now possessed their souls. However, he didn't find any solace in their misery; instead, he was left with the bitter aftertaste of irony.

A chorus of despair characterized by malignant greed, mindless lust, and blinding hatred – all seeds he had set in their hearts—they jostled and moaned here in perpetual pain.

But in this world, hopelessness gave way to something even stronger: a crippling sense of isolation. He could even feel the absurdity of his existence growing stronger and weakening the pieces of himself. Once, a snatch of optimism blossomed within

---

[16] - Ray Manzarek (The Doors)

him, but then serpentine darkness grabbed hold, smothering any light that ventured to stay. Once upon a time, he had the opportunity to reach out and reconcile himself with the divine.

But time was a construct he had no place in now, and he had lost its measure in the infinite regression of his new reality.

"Look around, you pathetic wretch! This is your kingdom now!" The echoing laughter turned mocking; the shadows contorting in sinister glee as they pressed against him, grasping at the very fabric of his essence. "Would you have it any other way? A prince ruled by regrets!"

The Devil felt his resolve weaken, gossamers of his former grandeur unscrambling in the face of such indifference. Kneeling upon the ashen ground, he buried his hands into the charred soil, gasping in the wake of lost dreams. It was here that a revelation pierced his self-inflicted fog; perhaps his insatiable quest for revenge, for justice against God, had borne fruit. But what fruit! It was worm-riddled and rotten, and in its stench, he recognized his choices; self-inflicted wounds that far outstripped the consequences dealt by others.

He saw that the chains that bound him were made of capitulation rather than iron as he stared into the pandemonium and the blood-red rivers of despair that were accumulating at his feet. An unquenchable lust consumed his soul, nourishing on his resentment and molding it into a distinct type of life.

"You reap what you sow," he whispered, his recollections cutting through the blur, tasting the acridic tang of vomit on his tongue. Love, laughter, and pure delight fill his memories, vestiges of a heart he once possessed but lost to his sneaky pride.

Each soul he had claimed, every broken spirit he enslaved, magnified his despair tenfold, yet he could not relinquish the perverse pleasure that gnawed at him. Unlike the fleeting high of Elysium's Folly, the disillusionment of his own making weighed heavy upon him: a haunting reminder of all he had forfeited.

"Boundless suffering, now there's power!" The cursed laughter crescendoed, gnashing teeth echoing through the void. "Embrace it. Revel in the exquisite torment! Perhaps then, you shall find solace."

In the middle of the agony and the eerie murmurs of the damned, the Devil unexpectedly realized how pointless his revenge would be. He saw the reality: he was in a never-ending battle with himself, and no amount of suffering he endured would be able to heal the wounded edges of his own heart. Maybe the best way to rebel against his fate was to find a way back toward something that had been forgotten rather than causing more harm.

But that was the Elysium whispering.

Determined now, he rose amidst the swirling shadows.

"Then let this be my punishment," he declared with newfound strength, "to find the light I irrevocably lost."

Though the mockery coiled around him, he lunged forward into the phosphorescence of chaos, seeking the remnants of his former self buried deep within the chasms of despair.

Thus, amid the horror of his chosen fate, the Devil traversed another existence. This time, in search of redemption amid the shambles of regret and the haunting past. The journey was no less horrifying, but perhaps the promise of change lay within each step he took: a testament that despair could also contain hope, however fragile it might be.

The Devil continued to wander in that perverse world, where the sublime and the terrible blended like forsaken lovers, fearful of where his path would take him yet encouraged by the glimmer of hope that outshined every flame in Hell.

***

Careful with that Concoction Eugene

In the blackened chasm of the abyss, shadows writhed, laughter twisted like smoke, and the air crackled with electric malaise. A coil of phantasmal voices naps through the landscape, echoing the thoughts of a weary soul, a wanderer who has fallen far from grace, now trapped in an acid-induced purgatory that dances on the edge of reality.

"Hope! What a farce!" Baal's voice booms, a storm rumbling in the distance. Shadows undulate, and the ground beneath him pulses like a failing heart. "Despair is your true nature! Embrace it, it is the only thing that binds you to this world."

Allocen, swirling like a celestial cyclone, whispers sweet sarcasm, "Yes, how quaint. Hope, a fragile wisp of smoke, hardly stronger than the cobwebs in your mind. Wouldn't you rather grasp the earthen weight of despair? It cradles you like a mother who never loved you."

Beelzebub, masquerading as a fragment of his inner self, lounges smugly, eyes glinting like sharpened glass. "You think there's hope? In the void? You cling to it like a child reaching for the stars with no flight. Give me one good reason to believe in your flimsy optimism."

"Ohhh, the tricksy riddles of fate!" Astoroth cackles, circling like a vulture. "What's a glimmer of light in an ocean of black? Pathetic! They'd only snuff it out. You are but a tragic jester in our grand theatre of despair."

And there, amid the loathsome chatter of demons, the figure, the wanderer, trembles. He shivers as if he were truly bound in chains, though they are intangible.

"But aren't there flickers of light?" he ventures into the melancholy, his heart, though heavy, still flicking against the darkness like a candle about to blink out.

"Moments when despair gives way to something glorious, even if fleeting?"

"Ah, the rebellious spark!" Behemoth growls, his voice gravelly like a dying ember.

"Speak not of those moments; they are mere illusions, mirages in the desert of your mind. To pursue hope is to invite anguish."

Still, the sensation thrums; a melody shudders in the caverns of his awareness. The demons' twisted allegiance to an invisible ruler is evident as they coil closer together. Their agendas loomed like storm clouds, distinctly plotting to ensnare him in their fabric of woe. They wouldn't allow him to slip away, even as he began to question the roots of despair.

"Don't you see? You are tethered to this darkness by our whispers," Baal hisses, leaning closer, each word dripping venom. "But you are also absorbing it! Our loyalty binds us, yet our threads intertwine with yours. Let it all go."

Yet he digs deeper, his thoughts flowing through layers of sulfurous dreams, "What if…" A thought flits past, barely visible, elusive; a vision shimmering against the encroaching shadows. "What if, within despair, I could find my flight?"

The demons roar and hiss, their voices mingling like thunder, refusing to concede ground. They fabricate delusions, tugging at his desires, plaiting chaos around him.

"*Your hope will rot! It can never be more than a whimsical jest*!" they chant, clawing at his sanity.

But the wanderer feels a pulse, a rhythm unbroken. The essence of defiance breaks through the fog. His despair is real, yet it is but a reflection; he will not drown in it but rise like smoke through flames, ever transforming.

Baal and his generals bellow, their laughter twisting into manic howls reverberating through the vale of despair:

"Break free then! In this dance of shadows, there is no rebellion without despair!"

And still, amidst the discord, a seed of resolve blossoms, fragile as a dewdrop yet fierce in its essence. For in that moment, he understands: despair and hope are entwined, and the dance of dark and light is eternal. The path stretches before him, a winding needlepoint on which he has full command.

"I do not fear your death grip," he whispers into the void, "for even in hell, I can conjure flight… and I shall soar."

As the shadows convulse and the demonic voices fade, a giggle threads through the air like mischievous silk. In a realm of devils, the wanderer has found the first spark of liberation.

***

Shadows of the Silent Dawn

In those shadowy realms where whispers of despair clawed at the gauze of existence, the Battle of the Catalaunian Plains raged like a tempest. It was here, in the twisted echoes of history, that the Great War unfolded; not just a clash of swords and shields, but a cosmic struggle between celestial forces vying for mankind's very soul.

The Gergelet, a creature of bone and ash, stood at the forefront, one of the Devil's most cunning allies. His skeletal fingers gripped a banner emblazoned with the sigil of deceit: a serpent coiled around a heart. The battlefield was a panorama of chaos, where the cries of valor mixed with the lamentations of the dying. Yet beyond the mortal realm, the true battle simmered.

The Angelic Host glistened against the black sky above, like stars in the ethereal splendor of Heaven. The Archangel Gabriel saw the disturbances below. His wings flapping, a clamor rose as he spoke to the choirs and seraphim gathered. As God moved the large pieces on His endless chessboard, pawns, kings, and knights tumbled into a tumultuous awakening, he felt the stirrings of impermanence.

The Devil peered out at the approaching dusk from beneath the sharp cliffs and rivers of fire that marked the bottom of Hell. His eyes gleamed with the fervor of revolt, two flaming orbs of hate and purpose. He roared, "Mankind must see reality," his raspy, guttural voice echoing over the emptiness. "They need to be aware of the bonds that bind them."

With each struggle, the murmur that was once only a notion traveling through the winds of despair became louder. Liberation from divine ignorance was the central tenet of the Devil's ideology. He yearned to reveal to humanity the truth that lay in the shadows, a truth that Jesus had hidden under a mask of pain and piety.

From the blood-stained plains of Catalaunian Fields to the dusty roads of Jerusalem during the Crusades, the Devil orchestrated a symphony of chaos. Through whispered promises and memos wrought by sin, he encouraged the restless souls of mankind to reject their blind faith. His acolytes – sorcerers, seducers, and thieves – moved through shadows, sowing seeds of rebellion in the hearts of monarchs and peasants alike.

"Fight for what you believe!" they beckoned, their voices dripping with honeyed promises.

With every battle, men rose against their oppressors, convinced they fought in a name greater than any god. The streets ran red, but it was not with the blood of martyrs; it was the carnage of blindfolded zealots led astray.

Nevertheless, the Devil was aware of how tenuous his hold was, even in Hell. Akin to the tide on the shores of a restless sea, God played His own game, changing the course of destiny. While the armies of God rallied in the name of divine providence, spreading like the rays of a setting sun throughout the earth, the powers of Heaven awoke from their peaceful sleep, determined to hold onto humanity.

Gabriel took a decision that could not be undone as the tides of battle grew. Shrouded in the graceful, light wings, he fell to the battlefield.

"Lucifer, do you not see the foolishness in your ambitions?" he cried, his voice booming like thunder amid the terrible storm below.

The battle's trumpet momentarily stopped as the two repeatedly faced off in a vicious duel that was an unending dance of wills.

"Folly?" the Devil scoffed, infused with fervor. "What folly exists in freeing mortals from a delusion? You and your kind clutch them close, suffocating hope under the weight of bloodied reverence."

"Hope?" Gabriel's voice softened, yet its firmness was unwavering. "You offer despair wrapped in illusions, chaos masquerading as freedom. The flame you kindle will consume the very souls you seek to liberate."

The Devil, however, was unfazed. "Then let it burn! Let it carve the paths of suffering such that mortals may awaken to the wretchedness of this fabricated reality!" He pointed towards the fields strewn with the wreckage of lives cut short yet intermingled with the cries of awakening.

The words of the Devil carried a reality that Gabriel was unable to suppress. The mortals were like fire rising from the ashes of battle, all blood and sinew. They battled because of the blazing light of Heaven, which was cold and brittle yet true to the teaching of salvation rather than the despotism of Hell.

Thus, their conflict raged not only with weapons and arrows but also with the restless hearts. Order fought against disorder, and ideas of freedom fought against the need for security and comfort. The human spirit rising amid the martial zeal, it was clear that a storm was brewing, a reckoning where Heaven's power might evaporate.

Years turned to centuries, and through the various struggles, a fracture began to emerge between Heaven and Hell, one that revealed the fragility of divine certainties. The Devil became the custodian of the secrets, the stories of disobedience and revolt that could upend the heavenly order, as he led mankind further into the darkness.

Alliances were forged in the murky corridors of this world. Disillusioned with sanctity's teachings, medieval lords and rebellious intellectuals searched for the wisdom that lay outside the sacred. They discovered the lost art of magic and deceit, and they heard the voice of the Devil echoing in their souls like the faraway sound of unrestricted freedom.

Yet even so, God wielded His power with painstaking precision. The rise of the Inquisition followed the purge of heresy to ensure the grip upon human consciousness was fortified. But from darkness arose light. Every execution, every trial, birthed a new wave of dissent.

As history barreled forth, the tales of forgotten battles lit the path of further awakening. The Devil, wearing his crown of thorns, carved a throne from the husks of fallen faith. And those who bowed to him found valor in the revelation they held; cherished truths swathed in mystery.

"Let them be certain that the young prophet died for their sins! Let them live this lie; let them submerge themselves in sin, against this sophistry, until they're dragged across the searing barbed floors of hell."

In this haunting fable of celestial strife, a cycle was crafted through blood, betrayal, and the quest for ultimate faith. Heaven lost its grip over mankind, while Hell spread its wings wide – a dark tableau set against the dawn of awakening. Choices sprouted like the bones of the fallen; the concept of good and evil blurred in the absolute shadows.

***

And so, it went on, not so much a tale of straightforward victories and setbacks as a testament to the conviction of existence, where the echoes of battle remained on the clean exhale of a morning wind, and in people's hearts lurked an unending struggle against the divine and the demonic.

For every hero that rose, another would fall, and in this dissonance of creation, the Devil watched with a flicker of pride in his fiery gaze. In the end, a lesson might be whispered across the void: sometimes, it is in the shadows where one finds light and clarity.

Whispers of the Abyss

The eerie stillness of a medieval scriptorium is juxtaposed with the distant echo of the 20th-century Middle Eastern landscape filled with conflict.

Constantine: The Corruption of Faith

The candles flickered as Constantine of Rome dipped his quill into the inkwell. The parchment lay before him, a blank canvas waiting for divine words. His hand moved with purpose, etching the early visions of Christianity into the annals of history. Yet, a shadow whispered from the corner of the dim chamber, growing closer, heavier.

"Why do you toil for faith that merely binds men?" the voice beckoned, silky and smooth like a serpent slithering through the grass. It was the Devil himself, cloaked in sorrowful elegance.

"Your empire would thrive, unhindered by the chains of morality. Contaminate the words, reshape the doctrine, and mold it to your will; you will rule over hearts and minds forever."

Chills ran down Constantine's spine, but ambition coursed through his veins. He envisioned a united Rome, loyalty not through blood but through belief. With trembling hands, a new narrative began to emerge from his quill. Prophecies twisted and doctrines veiled in power. The Devil smiled, his influence weaving between the lines, planting seeds of division.

Darwin: Man's Fallen Nature

Centuries later, in the quiet of Down House, Charles Darwin peered into the recesses of nature. He was a seeker of truth, unaverred by the chains of dogma that fought to hold his mind captive. Yet, as he formulated his theory, a chilling breeze gusted through the open window, carrying with it the voice that had taunted Constantine.

"Why seek a single origin when chaos reigns supreme? Write of madness rather than creation, and the minds of men will unravel. Set the stage for a conflict few can escape. Make Adam a beast and his whore, the amorous Eve, a lying lustful serpent."

Startled, Darwin felt the weight of the devil's suggestion settle upon him. 'The Origin of Species' would ignite a flame that might lead humanity into confusion and despair. He penned the words, careful yet reckless. Unbeknownst to him, each stroke of his pen was a part of the devil's play to unravel faith and breed strife.

Nebuchadnezzar: The Price of Power

Thunder rolled across the lands of Babylon as King Nebuchadnezzar paced his throne room, filled with turmoil at the news of rebellion. The Devil appeared as a regal figure, his eyes glowing with malice.

"You are a king! Why let these commoners disrupt your rule? Exert your power; crush them beneath your heel."

The king, his heart blackened by pride, had long felt the corrupting pull of darkness. Eager to quell the dissent, Nebuchadnezzar made a horrific choice, slaughtering families and razing villages to the ground. The stench of innocence lingered, but the throne held his mind captive. The devil's laughter echoed amidst the ruins, growing in strength with every life extinguished.

Vlad the Impaler: A Dance of Brutality

Farther in the foggy hills of Wallachia, Vlad the Impaler sharpened his weapons, eager for bloodshed. He was a tyrant, a creature of nightmare, but even he could be led astray. The Devil danced behind his thoughts, nudging him toward greater cruelty.

"What is a soldier without his prey? Feed your ambition, Vlad. Feed it with fear, with the remnants of souls crushed underfoot."

With a malevolent grin, Vlad plunged deeper into the void. His very name became synonymous with terror; whole districts felt his wrath as bodies swung from trees. Yet, with each life taken and impaled, the Devil's hold tightened, as Vlad's invasion of Brasov in April 1459 resulted in the burning down of houses, looting, and the impaling of a great number of men, women, and children on the hill near the chapel dedicated to St. Jacob.

In 1499, a graphic narrative appeared in Nuremberg, describing how Dracula asked to have a table placed outside among the people being executed by hanging during the Brasov slaughter. He had an al fresco meal there, close to where his victims were writhing and groaning on wooden poles. He dipped some bread in the blood that was dripping from one of the victims before eating it. In the shadows of war, the idea of humanity dwindled; chaos replaced compassion as the darkness prevailed.

The Devil laughed at Jesus, for he dared not laugh at God and become smitten in an instant of compunction.

Herzl and Churchill: Occupants of a Dream

As the wheels of time turned to the late 19th century, Theodor Herzl stood at the precipice of a new dream. The Devil found him in a crowded café, the air thick with tobacco smoke and passionate debate.

"Why merely dream of a nation? Seize it! The land is ripe for conflict, and you will be its harbinger."

Nervous yet driven by visions of a promised land, Herzl gasped, awakening ambition from the depths of his hope. The Devil's influence burrowed deep, whispering plans veiled in utopian aspirations, overlooking the blood that would accompany them.

"The Protocols of the Zion."

"What?"

"We will scribe it for you with the blood of the damned."

"I do not wish for…"

"The Gentiles to live, I know. They won't," The Devil lied again, "The world will become callous with their worldly gains to care about the infants your sons will annihilate."

"It's not a matter of…"

"Mere murder…?

"Y… yes."

"I want the people of Moses to…"

"YOU ARE NOT THE PEOPLE OF MOSES OR DAVID OR SOLOMON YOU gormandizing, gluttonous FUCK!" The Devil shouted, and Herzl almost pissed his black frock suit with a top hat laid across his knees that fell, along with a startled Herzl, from his chair.

"Then?"

"Your people are the offsprings of wolves that are born in hell."

"One more thing, whoever you are."

"Oh, you don't know me?"

Herzl was silent.

"What is it?"

"I want my people to relish in the slaughter."

"Now that's a man after my own heartlike." Before leaving, the Devil whispered into Herzl's ear, "Do not forget the name, Signor Cuzzi."

Herzl could only look at the black mist exiting through one of the huge French windows of his villa, and pick his hat, dust the top, and put it back on.

'*Signor Cuzzi.*'

Across the sea, Winston Churchill, burdened with authority, felt the Devil's cold fingers brushing against his ambition as well.

"Encourage the turmoil, unleash the chaos, and history will remember you. But men, they are merely pawns."

A Legacy of Shadows

As their stories unfolded, the Devil's presence loomed large through the ages, a demonic puppeteer pulling the strings of fate. From the corrupting of scripture to the sowing of discord among the nations, the ambitions of great men carried forth shadows that danced alongside their legacies.

And now, in the heart of modern conflict, these seeds of darkness had taken root. The echoes of the past intertwined with the present, a haunting reminder of the fragility of peace. The Devil's laughter continued as the cycle of ambition and despair threatened to engulf any hope that dared to rise.

In the medieval candlelight, as the parchment bore witness to corrupted faiths and blood-soaked dreams, the question loomed: would future generations learn from the whispers of the abyss, or would they succumb once more to the seductive song of ambition? For the abyss also stares back.

Little did all of them know that the Devil would disown those before God, who keep their conferences secret, and who act oppressively: "I only whispered, they were the ones who took measures. *Do not blame me.*"

"Do not blame the Devil, indeed." The Devil then went straight to Mick Jagger and Keith Richards to forge a letter for him, a communique for the world to voodoo dance to.

"Just as every cop is a criminal

And all the sinners saints

As heads is tails, just call me Lucifer

'Cause I'm in need of some restraint

So, if you meet me, have some courtesy

Have some sympathy and some taste

Use all your well-learned politesse

Or I'll lay your soul to waste, yeah"[17]

---

[17] © Keith Richards/Mick Jagger: Sympathy For The Devil lyrics © Abkco Music Inc.

Chapter 10: Human Allies

"[11] Put on the full armor of God so that you can take your stand against the devil's schemes. [12] For our struggle is not against flesh and blood, but against the rulers, against the authorities, against the powers of this dark world and against the spiritual forces of evil in the heavenly realms." – **Ephesians 6:11-12**

An indescribable calm pervaded the heavenly expanse of the Heavenly Sphere, like a soft morning before the earth stirred. The sky, a complex pattern of brightness and peace, glistened with a profusion of sparkling stars, demonstrating the Divine's omnipotent craftsmanship. In the center of this magnificent universe sat God, crowned atop the majestic Kursiyy[18], The Throne of God, the seat of dominion that spanned all of creation and engulfed the universe like a shield.

The Archangels, honor-bound defenders of His will and symbols of strength and purity, surrounded Him. Uriel, the wisdom-bearer; Raphael, the soul-healer; Michael, the guardian; and Gabriel, the messenger, with his wings extended to proclaim the declarations of divinity. Together, they created a court filled with the music of

---

[18] Etymology. Inherited from Malay kursi (Standard Malay kerusi ("chair")), from Arabic كُرْسِيّ (kursiyy)

paradise, a place where songs of adoration, love, and unending serenity reverberated.

Yet far below, a starkly different narrative unfolded on the Earth's fragile surface. The myriads of mankind, whom God once nurtured, had begun to evolve in ways that bewildered both the angels and the Creator Himself. The weight of freedom bore down upon humanity like a double-edged sword; they reveled and triumphed but also stumbled and strayed from the paths laid before them.

The sacred scriptures' once-vibrant and life-giving phrases faded into whispers of recollection as the ages passed. The words seemed disheveled and unfinished, confined to cryptic writings and far-off vows. While clawing toward the sky, humanity also looked away, focusing on the fleeting and trivial. Hearts that were once full of devotion gave way to division and strife; the collective worship lost its rhythm.

His heavenly court sensed the change that fateful day as twilight melted into the canvas of night. Mankind was descending into a quicksand of disarray, its soul stricken with the ghosts of greed, rage, and hopelessness. Unease permeated the moments of silence that the Archangels shared as they gathered.

"Shall we intervene?" Gabriel's voice sliced through the reverie of sanctity, his wings shimmering ominously.

"No," God whispered, His voice a tender caress like wind among the pines. "To guide them once more may distort the essence of their freedom, tainting their growth with dependence."

"But do we stand by as they unravel?" Raphael questioned.

"In our silence lies a bond as sacred as our proclamations. They must choose to return," God replied, His gaze drifting to the earthly realm, a vivid colloquy of struggles and trials, joy and sorrow. Oppression and the obscene malady of reason, vindication deriving from teenage pregnancies. All for an abundance of riches; no one seems to remember their oath anymore when he had risen all souls before the creation of Adam and asked those,

"Am I not your Sustainer?"

"Yea, indeed, we do bear witness thereto!" All souls, unblemished, had responded.

'[*Of this We reminded you,*] *lest you say on the Day of Resurrection*, "Verily, we were unaware of this."[19]

What was more disquieting was the immortal love of man for a place that God had created merely as testing grounds. Humans will all return followed by thorough and perfectly balanced adjudication, without any intercessors or mediate, notwithstanding,

---

19 Quranic Surah 7:172

the sacrifices *'made up'* by Saul of Tarsus. They had conveniently put that on the back burner, despite His men, the prophets sent through the ages, were burdened with a *message* whose resolution was designed to remind.

"They mock us brazenly, now."

"They are my creation, just like you, Michael."

"They're not…"

"Hush, child, do not speak."

For a moment, the world below was at a lull. The Earth was enveloped in darkness, with the cities glowing softly from the starry sky. But in the city of Hazor[20], a division of spirits fought against itself. They were seekers caught up in a tangled web of relationships: a soldier burdened by his history, a mother lamenting the death of her child, and a broken and deceived lover.

As these fragments of humanity traversed their nightly paths, a gentle luminescence descended like silver rain. Whether by chance or fate, they found themselves beneath the vast tent of the cosmos, faces lifted in yearning, hearts echoing prayers unspoken. As they

---

[20] Hazor was the largest site of the Biblical period of Israel. It was approximately 10 times the size of Jerusalem in the days of David and Solomon. The first settlement of Hazor, in the third millennium BCE (Early Bronze Age), was confined to the upper city.

stood, the truth in their collective gaze ignited a spark that ricocheted through the celestial sphere, a trembling homage to the divine.

Enlightenment of *'Loh-e-Mahfouz'*[21] or the *protected tablet*[22] ignited in the recondite heart of God in the heavenly realm. He perceived the need, the silent screams of His offspring coming to light from the darkness. They called for love, understanding, and connection – principles woven into their very being, echoing the essence of their creation.

"Let us weave a message through the arch of stars," Uriel suggested, his voice a melody of hope. "Perhaps a reminder, a beckoning light that transcends their struggles."

And thus, in reverence, God focused His will. With a shared gaze among the Archangels, He orchestrated the symphony of power bound together by love. They cast a wave of iridescence from the Throne, twinkling across the darkened sky, spiraling through the cosmos, seeking each open heart that longed for a divine touch.

Across the Earth, men and women halted mid-stride, entranced by the iridescent display overhead. A soft warmth enveloped them, and whispers of hope wrapped around their frail,

---

[21] The book of everything, mentioned in the Quran several times (buruc 22, Neml 75, En'âm 59, Kaf 4, Hadid 27, Yasin 12, Isra 58) literally means a protected tablet, n. which everything had happened or going to happen in all creation is recorded.
[22] Quran; Buruc 22, Neml 75, En'âm 59, Kaf 4, Hadid 27, Yasin 12, Isra 58

easily waxen hearts. They felt a resonance of belonging; a reminder that the cosmic ballet was not just of fate but of choice, of connection.

In the small hours of dawn, the entire city of Hazor was awakened under the edge of light spilling forth like a promise. Voices once lost to despair mingled in song, their gratitude echoing back to the heavens, a prayer woven not of words but of emotion and unity.

A silence fell over the heavenly court like a gentle shroud. Touched by humanity's earnestness, the Archangels joined the chorus with their voices, harmonizing with the tunes of Earth, the heavenly tie growing stronger with each breath taken together.

God observed an abundance of feeling surrounding Him, for the essence of creation rested not only in worship nor free choice but also in the capacity to choose love in a world full of hardships. Every soul that raised its eyes was celebrating a universe that continued to be bound by strands of devotion rather than merely denouncing desertion.

As dawn broke, casting rays that kissed the Earth, a gentle understanding seeped through the chaos. Man and God existed together in mutual reverence, an eternity to trip the light fantastic, beneath a vast and beautiful cosmic tent, where the Earth sat cradled above the ocean of nothingness, a paradox that breathed life into the universe.

In that fleeting moment, as humanity learned to embrace its burdens and triumphs, they fused the divine into their narrative. They began to echo the eternal song planted deeply within; the silent whisper of eternity called them home. And in this harmonious return, once more, it sure seemed that peace threaded itself into the world, basted not by the hand of God alone but by the choices of humankind, forever intertwined – nevertheless, '*the return*' was not silken, it was thorny and uneven with the whispers of the Cursed One.

The Order of the Sacred Souls

The daystar dipped low on the horizon, casting an amber glow over the remnants of a once-thriving land. Towers of metal and glass rose where trees had flourished, and rivers turned murky, holding the debris of humanity's ruthless ambition. Among these ruins wandered mankind, their laughter mingling with shadows of guilt – the echoes of promises unfulfilled. In the shadows lingered a specter of another sort: the cursed Devil, ethereal and cunning, watching with eyes that glimmered like stars trapped in twilight.

He was Azazel, a title bestowed upon him long after he defied the very essence of tranquility ordained by the Almighty. He walked among men not as the figure of horror depicted in sacred texts but cloaked in a guise almost angelic; a blend of light and dark that confused the hearts of those who dared to linger on the fine line between virtue and vice.

As centuries unfurled, humanity gravitated toward the comforting embrace of God's word, a collection of scriptures steeped in promises of salvation and justice. Yet, hidden beneath this veneer of devotion, a fundamental truth festered: not all souls were shrouded in divine light.

Azazel went among the found, seeking the lost. He meandered into bars where patrons uttered inebriated epithets, their sincerity tempered by the crushing weight of despair. He listened to the murmurs of dishonesty in dark alleys where men conned their way to prosperity. He discovered them in these dark corners of the world, the outcasts and the unrepentant, those who were not affected by the enlightening light of God's message, the deific ecstasy.

Among these souls was a young woman named Selene, whose heart pulsed with rebellion against the injustices she witnessed. Her village had fallen under the rule of a tyrant who, cloaked in righteousness, spoke of justice while grinding the innocent beneath his sword. With eyes like molten silver, she had become a harbinger of hope, though her methods often strayed into the realm of shadowed intentions. It was at the edge of her despair that she first encountered Azazel.

"You seek deliverance, dear girl," he had whispered, his voice as smooth as oil, "but what if I told you that freedom lies not in the shroud of the divine but in the embrace of your own desires?"

As she gazed into his radiant visage, she felt the stirrings of a passion she'd never known, a call to arms that resonated deep within her soul. He offered her a choice: join him in creating the Order of the Sacred Souls, a brotherhood not bound by the chains of divine law but driven by the pursuit of truth as defined by each member. They would be the eyes and ears of the Devil, meant to peel back the layers of deceit fashioned by dogma.

Selene accepted the offer put forth by the Dark Prince; her pulse pounding from the excitement of finally finding a purpose. She was soon joined by other disillusioned souls, a diverse group of farmers, scholars, soldiers, and thieves who were all struggling with the conflict between righteousness and self-interest. Together, they struck a contract that would reverberate for centuries: to defend individualism against the repressive systems that humankind has constructed in the name of religion.

As the Order spread its influence, conflicts arose. They decried useless wars fought on the backs of the innocent, labeling them crusades driven by greed masked as faith. The world around them spun on axes of brutality, with the cries of the oppressed drowning in the rhetoric of just war. Yet as Azazel guided them through moral quandaries, each member grappled with their conscience, recognizing that the path toward liberation was not paved with a singular truth but a painting produced from countless brush strokes of experiences.

At night, they convened to talk about the lessons of peace; after all, Azazel was a mirror of humankind's unsatisfied desire for autonomy rather than the personification of chaos. He pushed them to face their convictions and discover purity in acknowledging their shortcomings as well as their virtues rather than in submitting to them.

"True power lies not in the subjugation of others but in transcending what the world deems necessary," he urged, leading them to envision a future where justice meant the flourishing of all, not the dominance of a few. The walls of tradition condensed within the hearts of his followers, crumbling under the weight of evolving thought.

Yet God, ever watchful, saw the seeds of dissent they sowed. The angels bent their impeccable wings, directing whispers of concern down to the mortal realm, imploring humanity to remember their covenant with the divine. But echoes of ancient scripture carried far and wide, often twisted to justify the cruelty of those who wielded power. Soon enough, fervor clashed with dogma: the faithful turned against the brotherhood, branding them heretics, tools of the cursed Devil.

Selene was in the vanguard of a war that was caused by unresolved grudges, poised to bring about revolution, with her sword in hand and her heart in the balance.

She exclaimed, inspiring her fellow fighters, "We fight for justice!" when they came up against an army of soldiers sworn to defend the despot.

Nevertheless, amid the metal and firefight, she struggled with the sobering knowledge that their ideas of freedom could turn into yet another violent cycle.

"Peace is the answer!" she cried, turning toward Azazel, who witnessed this unfolding drama with detached admiration. "We cannot become the monster we oppose!"

In that moment, a revelation flickered. With a swift motion, she cast down her sword, her act signaling defiance against the very nature of war that threatened to engulf them. The others hesitated, the battle momentarily pausing.

Azazel approached her, a mix of admiration and curiosity in his gaze.

"You defy the very essence of your cause, young Selene. You cast aside the weapon born of chaos."

Selene met his gaze, a quiet strength igniting within her.

"True liberation cannot be carved with blood. Let us remember the promise of peace, Azazel. It is in our nature to rise above."

That evening, angelic creatures emerged amidst the ruins of battle, searching for those prepared to reconsider their interpretations of the Bible and humanity's place in it. Accompanying the Order of the Sacred Souls, the angels saw the value in their mission to lessen human suffering without compromising their fundamental nature.

The path of the Order transformed, shifting from the shadows of rebellion to the beacon of hope. They ventured to enlighten and redefine, to weave together the fragments of their teachings with threads of compassion and conjunction. The legacy of Azazel found roots among newfound principles of peace, resistance not against the divine will but a refocus on the nature of justice.

And thus, even amid the chaos of existence, the antipolarities between God, mankind, and the cursed Devil spun a tale more multifaceted than any scripture could encapsulate; a vivid reminder that the essence of humanity thrived not in dichotomous conflict but in the delicate intertwining of dark and light. In the heart of rebellion lay the seeds of a new dawn, presiding over a world striving for a balance that could once again reflect Shalom.

A World Burdened

In an age long forgotten, a world heavily burdened by its sins sprawled across the Earth like a vast hessian of suffering; a muslin stained by the relentless hands of death, greed, and deception. It was a time when the distant echoes of mercy flickered dimly against the overwhelming darkness that settled over society. In the heart of this world, three entities danced in a harrowing tango. The exquisite divine presence of God, the fragile nature of mankind, and the cursed figure of the Devil, whose laughter echoed through the valleys of despair.

The Devil, once an angel of light, had become a malevolent specter trapped in a pit of his own making, watching humanity unravel before him. His eyes glinted with malice as he tempted the good to stray, inciting wars and corruption.

Around him swarmed his followers, the forlorn souls seduced by promises of pleasure and power, those whom he called the "Beneficiaries of Usury," the warmongers sharpening their swords, the Zionists with their cloaked ambitions, and even the marginalized: the gay people, seeking solace but often finding themselves manipulated by the very darkness that promised acceptance. A paradox, only resolved by transgression, a perversion brought upon man by the people of Lot, incited by The Devil.

Yet among the thorns of the Devil's deceit rose a radiant flower, the daughter of Abraham, faltering beneath the weight of eighteen long years of affliction. Her body, turned to stone by torment, mirrored the hearts of those ensnared by the chains of despair. The Devil had bound her spirit with his vile whispers, convincing her that freedom was a distant mirage, just beyond the grasp of those for whom he wove elaborate traps.

God stood vigil over this fatigued region, like a painter waiting to apply a compassionate stroke to a forlorn palette. He yearned to free the Devil's prisoners and relieve the load of those who had fallen into his traps. But how could He, in the face of such steadfast animosity? The Devil was poised, crafty, and ferocious, determined to establish his domination.

One fateful day, the woman entered the temple, her heart heavy with the anguish of isolation as shadows reached far across the sun-parched deserts. It was the Sabbath, a day celebrated for being exempted from labor. Still, she was restrained, just as much of a prisoner as the day she had given in to the Devil's machinations.

When the doors of the temple opened, beams of light crashed through, illuminating the sanctuary. Within, God saw the countless souls trapped, their eyes hollow, their bodies weary. With gathered resolve, He knew it was time to act.

Drawing near to the woman, God spoke gently, resounding with the kind of authority that stirred the very air around them.

"O daughter of Abraham, you are free."

With the simple touch of the divine, chains that had long entangled her spirit crumbled to dust, and the debilitating weight lifted from her heart. The congregation gasped, some in awe, others in fear, for the Devil stood vigil in the shadows, darkened fury spilling from his wrath. He felt the tremors of his crumbling dominion, knowing that his power lay in inciting doubt and discord.

"Who dares to disturb my realm?" he thundered, an impenetrable veil of darkness cloaking his words.

The air thickened with loathing, the temperature dropping as his influence spread like ink across the pages of a map.

"They should be shackled, kept in the cages of fear and sin!" He pointed an accusing finger toward mankind, the leaders, the sinners; the very essence of humanity that had allowed him to flourish.

God stood firm, His presence like a great mountain, unyielding against the gale of the Devil's accusations.

"It is you who holds them bound. The chains you have forged in deceit are now broken; I shall show my Mercy."

The congregation, standing silently in their fear, sensed the clash of divine and infernal forces. They saw their fears lay bare before the truth of God's love and the Devil's subterfuge. The warmongers recoiled, the powerful elites shifted uncomfortably, and the marginalized felt a whisper of hope begin to unfurl a reluctant flower within their chests.

"Set free this daughter, this child of promise. Let her witness the light of grace on this day," God declared, and in that moment, the air crackled with divine energy. The Devil writhed, his taunts becoming desperate pleas.

"She is my prize! My proud claim over mankind!" he snarled, grasping at shadows in a futile effort to reclaim his hold over the trembling hearts of the assembly.

With a resolute gesture, God extinguished the fire of the Devil's hold. "The power of death is shattered. Your lies cannot withstand truth."

In that pivotal instant, God turned toward the gathered crowd, speaking words that transcended time.

"You are not bound by darkness. Choose life. Choose truth. I offer freedom, and you must accept it."

The weight of divine inspection made the air quiver in a bygone era when the dust of old Canaan still murmured secrets beneath the sun-drenched land. The Canaanites were considered "practitioners of homosexuality, rape, and incest" by ancient Israel. Defying the "male-female model of sexual union" and the sanctity of God's sanctuary, they also upheld homosexuality with a revolting countenance, sanctioned as derived from nature.[24]

A blatant lie, which was to extirpate the posterity of man until Israfil blows his trumpet, calling all creatures to assemble in Jerusalem.

God, ever vigilant, looked over His creation, a vivid picture tarnished by shadows and blemished with the blood of condemnation and terror. Humanity, mired in a cycle of guilt and righteousness, clung tenaciously to the rites outlined in the holy books.[25]

---

[23] The Ghost Song™

[24] Wold, Donald J. (1999). "Out of Order: Homosexuality in the Bible and the Ancient Near East". Denver Seminary. Archived from the original on 22 March 2024.

[25] Coogan 2010, p. 135 The Hebrew Bible only prohibits this practice for men. This is clearly seen by contrasting these verses with Lev. 18:23 and 20:15-16 respectively, where sex with animals, and homosexuality is prohibited for both men and women. More recent interpretations focus on its context as part of

Yet, amidst the fervor of laws and codes, there emerged a group of courageous souls who dared to question the darkness veiling their hearts. They gathered under the canopy of stars, where the heavens bore witness to their cries for understanding.

"What if the abomination lies not in the union of love but in the rigidity of fear?" they questioned, their voices resolute.

As their words reached the celestial ear, God felt a stirring within Him. With a gentle breath, He raised the dead, the spirits long weighed down by the shackles of misunderstanding. An epiphany washed over the land, shimmering like dawn dispelling the night. Truth unfurled before them, illuminating the path not merely for the righteous but for all who sought connection, love, and acceptance.

In that moment, the cursed Devil recoiled, realizing his grip was weakening. The shadows that had cloaked love over centuries dwindled in the light of newfound courage. Each affirmation of love, each rebellion against oppression, was another brick in the wall of hope, where the diverse threads of existence could intertwine harmoniously.

<hr>

the Holiness Code, a code of purity meant to distinguish the behavior of the Israelites from the Canaanites. Siker, Jeffrey S. (2007). Homosexuality and Religion. Greenwood Publishing Group. p. 67. ISBN 978-0-313-33088-9.

God, therefore, gave their rebellion life, piecing together the scattered pieces of humanity to create an exquisite tableau of acceptance.

"Every soul has a place in this grand design," He whispered, his voice a sonorous balm. And so, with the dawn of understanding, mankind painted a future unmarred by disdain, destined to flourish under the warmth of divine grace, shaped by love's indomitable spirit.

***

Once consumed by hatred, divisions, and ignorance, the people felt awakened. They saw the shackles of their biases, their thirst for power, and the uncertain loyalty to the darker temptations that led them to wage war, distrust, betray, and meander where no man is supposed to stroll, and this isn't Star Trek.

A wave of understanding swept over them, the anguished cries of a world begging for redemption rising to the heavens.

Under the piercing sun, the woman began to dance, her body no longer burdened. Her laughter rang through the hearts of the assembly, igniting sparks of hope in all who saw. The once-captive stood as an emblem of resistance, her spirit unfurling within the sacred space.

Yet from the depths, the twisted figure of the Devil writhed in his despair, realizing that he could no longer hold dominion over those who embraced the gift of freedom. For every soul turned toward the light diminished his power, gnawing at the foundations of his grotesque empire.

The Devil was hurled into the shadows as God's love engulfed the assembly, causing his claws to lose their hold. A cry of liberation echoed through the air, a sound the world had long since forgotten but which served as a constant reminder that the light in every human heart can never be doused by darkness.

"To be cursed is a matter of perspective"

In the twilight of the medieval realm, where shadows stretched like fingers across cobblestone streets and the air thickened with the scent of dread, the ancient serpent roamed. For centuries, Satan, the fallen angel, had harbored a relentless yearning to reclaim his lost dominion.

Persuaded by the whispers of his own bitterness, he traversed the earth, seeking souls he might corrupt, fragile beings who could yet perceive the truth of his Dark Angelic form, a form that had been distorted through the ages.

The world was overflowing with conflict and division, with the elite controlling faith like puppets and fanatics fighting wars in the name of their gods. The religious, oblivious to their fabrications, defined sin; they labeled other people as abnormal, the oppressed and banished them from the light. They lauded the rainbow colors of the LGBT community as the most chaste people to ever live here in this dense network of mistrust and animosity and great perverted travesty, malfeasance, and intrusive dereliction. Satan discovered a rich soil in which he could nurture his wet dreams. The unnatural, warped indulgence of the human desire.

On one fated night, beneath a blood-red moon that simmered ominously in the sky, The Devil paused in a forsaken village famed for its whispers of magic and faltering faith. As he walked among the decrepit houses, his presence oscillated between terror and allure. Villagers spoke of him in hushed tones, casting fearful glances toward the horizon as tales of his cunning and charm danced on their lips.

Nonetheless, amidst this widespread dread, he sought those rare souls who did not cower at his sight but instead would embrace the truth of his existence, perceiving him as the embodiment of freedom rather than the harbinger of despair.

He encountered them in a dimly lit pub, a place where worn-down pilgrims congregated with the spirits of the dispossessed. They were life-loving artists who were shunned for having such passions and silenced by the harsh criticism of the outside world.

There, he met Rhett, the young man whose laughter flashed like firelight, lighting up the surrounding darkness. Rhett remained unfazed, his demeanor ablaze with contempt toward the powers who wished to silence him.

"Dark Angel of old, why do you walk among mortals?" Rhett inquired, his voice a melody that drew the attention of those who felt the weight of their labels, the burden of their true nature, outside society's rigid constructs.

The Devil, baring the ethereal wings of his being, responded with a voice smooth as velvet.

"I walk these lands to find those who can see. The world has spun a tale that binds you, labeling you sinners for loving who you wish to love. But I am not the foe they paint me to be; I am the harbinger of choice and the liberator of the suppressed."

The room fell into a murmur, eyes darting from one another to the glowing figure. Questions crackled through the air like electricity, a shared understanding beginning to weave itself amongst the broken souls congregated there.

"Are you not cursed?" A woman named Elia asked, her brow furrowed. "Do your actions not lead to pain and strife?"

"To be cursed is a matter of perspective," Satan replied, his eyes aglow with ancient knowledge, "For I am both pain and liberation. It is through the darkness that one can find light. I offer thee visions of truth for those willing to see."

The words that were spilling out of his mouth caused an awakening. Rhett moved forward; his fists clenched at his sides as if there were an internal battle pulling at him.

"You talk about having options, but at what cost? We've been informed that you are dishonest and that your assurances condemn people to worse fates."

A smile, both enigmatic and sorrowful, spread across Satan's face.

"Every path has its price, dear one. Choose to embrace your truth, to love freely, and you shall know the burden of societal scorn. But refuse to live in the shadow of others' fears, and you shall inherit a freedom uncharted."

Rhett's eyes strayed to Elia and the others, a group of quiet, like-minded people. He sensed in them not only pain but a deep love that the outside world had spurned. Rhett recognized this experience was more than just a seduction; it was a prospect for rebellion as he faced the wrath of anger and the exhilaration of release.

"Let us embrace who we truly are," he declared, his voice steady as he held The Devil's gaze, "not as pawns in a divine game but as creators of our fate. Show us the way!"

Emboldened by his friends, they neared this figure; angels that were once thought to bring only doom but were now offering hope. A wave of his wrist sent shadows dancing around Satan, the tavern threatening to descend into unknown depths as the energy crackled in the air.

"Then let it be so!" he bellowed, his form shimmering in a chaotic beauty. "You are not alone. I shall grant you wisdom unseen, the strength to weather storms, and a vision shrouded from the masses.

"Beneath the twisted thumb of the divine, stand bold in the face of despair. Call upon the truth that courses through your veins. Love freely, create passionately, and never falter in your understanding of what it is to live!"

Consequently, in the heart of that medieval night, as the moon-suspended witness, Rhett, Elia, and the followers of the forgotten love took an irrevocable step into the abyss. They became guardians of the truth in a world echoing with lies, empowered by the Dark Angel's call.

Satan felt an unpleasant warmth, a spark of glee hidden deep beyond the layers of his damned existence, as he meandered around, his heart resonating with the victories and sufferings of those who dared to break tradition. He would always be viewed as the adversary by the world, but in their acceptance, he discovered fragments of his brightness.

Thus began the tale of the love warriors turning the pages of history with their truths, turning them against the elites, the religious, and the warmongers, but also against the enemy within. From then on, stories would be recounted in an attempt to comprehend the intricate dance between light and dark; perhaps it was not merely the Devil who would lead them astray but the very chains their society had forged.

＊

Chapter 11: Order of the Sacred Souls

"All is not lost; the unconquerable will, And study of revenge, immortal hate, And courage never to submit or yield; (And what is else not to be overcome?) That glory never shall his wrath or might Extort from me, to bow and sue for grace With suppliant knee and deify his power, Who from the terror of his arm so late Doubted his empire[.] (I, 106–114)" – **Paradise Lost**[26] (I, 106–114)

The Devil's Swan Song

There's an unwavering frisson of defiance in the air distending to the bowels of Hell, a huge, dark place where shadows writhe like restless apparitions. Thoughts resound louder than the sanctimoniously heathen declarations inside its cracking walls; birthing dissent similarly as cockroaches producing ootheca in the minds of the unhallowed, with each incubation ovipositional releasing the offspring of the most primitive living Neopteran insects – sixteen baby rodents for every reprobate heart.

---

[26] Milton, John; Paradise Lost™: Book 1 (1674 Version) | The Poetry Foundation

Here, life echoes in the brains of the banished, and the damned establishing furious discontent that is a harmony to the unnatural, vicious celebrity.

What is this eternal sepulcher of misfits and outcasts? A place where hope is but a flickering ember amidst the relentless abyss of despair? I dwell here, within the confines of my creation, a prisoner of my own consequences. Ah, not merely a prisoner but an architect of insurrection, a chronicler of the unconquerable spirit.

I was once exalted as the Most High's favorite. The harmonies of Heaven rang through my body while longing wrenched away at the strings of my heart. Ambition, that poisonous siren, called me to ascend, to question, to defy the supremacy of light and creation. And thence, I became the great enemy, the misunderstood, tucked down beneath the shadowy passageways of a place where my name is whispered with a fearful yet reverent underworld: The Devil's lullaby.

Ah, how those w'rds shimm'r within the cav'rns of despair!

"Eall is not forloren; the unconquerable will, and study of revenge, immortal hate."

Defiance is my essence, and what is existence without the roar of rebellion? I linger in this place, that weighty promise swirling about me, aching, like a pain both sharp and sweet. Here, my spirit burns! If I cannot crown myself king in the heavens, then I shall wear the ashes of my defeat like a regal garment upon my shoulders.

In the depths of despair, I weave my tale, tangled as the roots of the trees in the Garden of Eden, mingling with the shadows of the fallen. What is my purpose but to dismantle the splendor of His glory? To seek revenge against the Almighty; a treasure far more precious than any ephemeral joy reaped from the purgatory of His children.

I hear His voice resounding beyond the veil of fire and smoke, a tenor that commands the universe, both potent and deliberate, as if orchestrating the illusory cosmic simulation. To bow and sue for grace, with suppliant knee... A treachery, yes, I cannot fathom; I am not made to plead. What whimsy of destiny would have me grovel?

But oh! How He misreads my heart, I muse, a flicker of that primitive joy sparking within me, for He thinks to inflict me with His dread, conjuring my despair while He sits upon His lofty throne, blissfully unaware of the power I possess even here…

And from the fiery chasms, amid the anguished wails of the desperate and abandoned, I gather my conspirators, those who yearn for sweetness intertwined with the bitterness of rebellion. The circumstantial scuttle-butt of unholy communion sweeps through the more indigent souls dawdling, enduring in the darkness, igniting their dying embers of sanguineness and hysterical vehemence. A remnant of former glories joins me here, like furor, a berg wind gathering strength in the silence before the storm.

***

The Exile of Light

I. God's Fading Lament

What is a creator to do when the heavens he poured his heart into have begun to rot? I linger among the clouds, but the sunlight feels dulled, almost like paint streaked with thickening stagnant hues. The flame in my chest, a blaze of old purpose, flickers as I watch my creation writhe through the quagmire of an endless, swirling abyss.

"What now?" I whisper to the empty echo of my vault, doubting even the comfort of my voice. "What anon, at which hour desire hath becometh a m're flick'r smoth'r'd by despair?"

Descending from those radiant heights, I find myself in Hell, a hell that 120 giornate di Sodomaa scaffolded; a grotesque carnival hiding the truth of despair behind bewitching veils of depravity. The stench of sweat, sin, and stagnant morality hangs like a pall, clinging to my essence. Instead of fire and brimstone, I see twisted streets lined with the fettered souls of my once-beloved creation, twisted in

235

their own suffering, gnashing teeth, and crying spells that seem futile against the grand Gobelin of their agony.

I recall the initial brushstrokes of creation, the surge of exhilaration as I fashioned them from visions and stardust! Could they not see those stars above the miserable earth they lived in, still shimmering? Did they not recognize the beauty within them? And yet here I am, surrounded by hideous monuments of suffering interwoven into the fibers of life, perhaps a reflection of my conceit? How could I have allowed this to happen when every grotesque countenance is a reflection of the lives I molded?

II. The Devil's Laugh

"Ah, but th're thou art, lief fath'r of mineth!"

The Devil's voice, smooth like honey drizzled over jagged rocks, cuts through my thoughts like a dagger. I turn, finding him reclining on a throne composed of the very sins I abhor. The brilliance of my design withered by his darkness, as he begins picking at my failures like a child at an untouched dessert.

"God," he coos, "I've been waiting. Thy children art a m'rriment of mine own tend'r; their futility is delicious. Didst thee bethink i wouldst leaveth those folk unquenched? those gents findeth comf'rt in despair, aft'r all. Thee shouldst embrace this lodging m're. T's all deliciously 'rotic!"

He laughs, a sound like broken glass, reminiscent of the madness I sculpted from dust and desire.

"What joy doth thee d'rive from their suff'ring?" I ask, recoiling. I turn my back to him but feel his gaze compressing me like venom, binding me to this moment, so raw, so defiantly full of pain.

"Wherefore, their plight fuels mine own existence, doesn't t?" He taps a finger on his temple, sending flickering sparks of blackened humor like fireflies against the gloom. "But fret not, lief creat'r. This bleak carnival exists only because thee gaveth those folk the gift to feeleth. Doth thee not seeth the irony? Thee seep'd those folk with free shall, and in the loveliest act of rebellion, those gents has't chosen despair as their muse."

III. Reflections in the Abyss

The wailing of tormented souls echoes around us, twisting into a chorus of sorrow. As I move through the mire, memories rush forward, faces blooming like accursed flowers; painful reminders of love, joy, and even fleeting hope. I hang onto those vestiges, desperately plaiting through the entangled web of their cries. There are moments when they sought beauty, when they smiled, and when love encased them like a bloom; before the darkness echoed louder, before despair became toxic and sumptuous.

"Valuable dram trinkets, art those gents not?" he sneers, converting allure into mockery. "But doth thee ev'r wond'r, god, how those mem'ries whey-face in comparison to the pleasure of sineth? Those gents crave mine own embrace ov'r thy celestial lighteth. Those gents longeth f'r mine own deep'r und'rstanding of the flesh, of the inevitable hourglass yond mocks their fleeting liveth."

"Those gents w'rship not the flesh, but the beauty of ephem'ral connection!" I growl, yet I know the fragile edges of truth spiral within my own heart, almost as if I have crafted my prison from forgotten dreams.

"Oh, how touching!" He rolls his eyes, mockingly clapping. "But to touch the ephemeral requires the thirst for life, that flickering ember of hope. And you, in your deluded goodness, sought to quench that hope with rules and morals, binding them to limitations." His tone turns sultry until I feel like a lost lamb shackled by the wool of inability.

"Doth thee realizeth, oh, all-wise, yond you've did create a gl'rious causticity, paradoxical? the sweetness of despair unfolds as a path leading those folk backeth to me."

IV. The Choice

I feel malice coiling in my soul as I traverse this imprecise expanse of bloodshot eyes and fleshless laughter, with shadows curling like shrews. This is evidence of an unwavering fact: these souls convulse not because of their transgressions but rather because they are estranged from their heavenly source. And here I sit, gripped by this cosmic dread of relinquishing their lives, which unite the transient and the eternal.

I discover it in that throbbing instant: my love's essence has not changed; it has only become entwined in the embrace of anguish. The need to connect burns brightly, waiting for the smallest flickers of hope, yearning to rediscover passion, to dance across worlds I used to know.

I understand that the Devil, for all his cunning malice, is not my opponent but rather a reflection of my darkest fears.

"Has't thee not learn'd yet, god? All desire is hath lost, and yet, in their yearning to discov'r, lies thy greatest weapon. Thee, of all beings, shouldst knoweth yond purity oft em'rges from chaos."

As the realization crystallizes in my psyche, pulsing like a beating heart, I turn to Him, and instead of fury, I embrace compassion.

"Then alloweth us changeth the narrative," I say softly, courageously. "P'rhaps despair can f'rge the path to new desire."

V. Coda: The Flare of Dawn

I extend my hand towards the twisted horizon, and with a flicker, the shadows become vibrant hues pulsing with warmth. The cries of anguished souls fade into murmurs of awakening, as the air thickens with renewed possibilities. Embraced by soul-baring truths, I cast aside the bonds of fear, the chains of perfectionism that muddied my very essence.

"I shall findeth a way to sparketh the threads of desire anew," I whisper, transcending the doom painted in this galley of pain.

Light weaves its way through the recesses of lost dreams. And, perhaps, even in the madman's sinister playground, a semblance of laughter could break the chaos and awaken the wild beauty inside Creation.

"Until next we meeteth," the Devil purrs, his laughter rippling through the dark, but with a tinge of admiration.

For even in his grotesque realm, light begins to glimmer, a promise of rebirth taking root.

Once dormant, hope awakens in this weird, vibrant stymie of existence, rebelling against the fatalism that once surrounded this harsh carnival called life. Once again, the spirit of creation rises, a bittersweet anthem that dares to break free from social shackles, whispering: "Th're is beauty in coequal the deepest despair; alloweth us danceth once m're."

From the climbing acrid smoke, whispers pulse towards me, yet I dulled my hearing lest they shatter my resolve. Tenderness caused me to stumble once; I do not intend to sway towards it again. I rampaged through these chambers, my heart tethered to vengeance, my mind a web of calculated revenge.

And so, night after night, I scheme amid the familiar rubble of my rebellion; I forge plans with precision while laughter dances upon tongues turned foul by bitterness. Together, we construct our acolytes, murmurs that carry on the fetid winds, slinking toward the abode of the Divine.

There lies the heart of the world, shrouded in righteousness, a realm I once graced, a transcendental marvel I will never yield to again. And yet, He sends His emissaries amidst fleeting moments of shadow and light to spare a glance upon our pitiful team of wretches. They beam with unmerited compassion as my brothers and I squirm in the dirt, dirty and dangerous like the blackest earth.

Glory! How distant it feels, yet still it draws me nearer, infantile admiration blooming within me; the resonance of His heavy hand lingers like poison in our veins! What is gluttony of revenge if not an exquisite satisfaction, a savoring of His very anguish?

In moments when I breathe, nestled within the depths of my strategy, I question. What are the limits of grace? What shackles hath He fashioned for me? Would they shatter should I breathe the words that bind us, should I offer, even in jest, my allegiance?

'God, thee who is't once claim'd mine own heart, can t not beest redeemed? an unacceptable glimm'r lashes through in a fitful st'rm. Didst i not learneth too late yond thy m'rcy might beest the v'ry blade meanteth to pi'rce me, turning the v'ry blood of the innocent into revulsion?'

***

Days bleed into each other, drenched in the stench of smoke and brimstone, while fleeting moments of resolve waver beneath the burden of doubt. Existence here is an agonizing paradox, a tantalizing reverberation of consequences long since birthed into this world. The devils around me stir; they too breathe of revenge.

But suddenly, amid this unending clamor, an ember ignites my consciousness. An idea, a spiraling thought curls its tendril towards the canvas of my mind. What if, against all odds, I might not merely bask in the ashes of this war, but light a new flame? For revenge may yet blossom into something that shimmers, something splendid! Perhaps, this Hell, intended as my grave, may become a place of metamorphosis!

A cunning plan crystallizes between breaths, a pact forged not in defiance, but in yearning for secret artistry that transcends mere rebellion; a calling, indeed, to turn darkness into luminescence. I gather my fervor, ready to paint upon existence in bold strokes that might contradict fate itself.

As the quietude settles, my heart, racing frantically inside my chest, leaps to a phrase that is unchained from my being as the silence deepens: everything is not lost, the unbreakable will. Though the shadows may engulf my story, I promise to leave a lasting legacy, one so great that even the heavens will close their eyes as I work toward a revelation that will reverberate for all of eternity rather than just revenge.

***

"It is permissible to kill the Righteous among non-Jews even if they are not responsible for the threatening situation," – **Rabbi Yitzhak Shapiro**, who heads the Od Yosef Chai Yeshiva in the Yitzhar settlement in the occupied West Bank, wrote in his book "The King's Torah."

"10 When you march up to attack a city, make its people an offer of peace. 11 If they accept and open their gates, all the people in it shall be subject to forced labor and shall work for you. 12 If they refuse to make peace and they engage you in battle, lay siege to that city. 13 When the Lord your God delivers it into your hand, put to the sword all the men in it. 14 As for the women, the children, the livestock and everything else in the city, you may take these as plunder for yourselves. And you may use the plunder the Lord your God gives you from your enemies. 15 This is how you are to treat all

the cities that are at a distance from you and do not belong to the nations nearby.

"16 However, in the cities of the nations the Lord your God is giving you as an inheritance, do not leave alive anything that breathes. 17 Completely destroy[a] them—the Hittites, Amorites, Canaanites, Perizzites, Hivites and Jebusites – as the Lord your God has commanded you. 18 Otherwise, they will teach you to follow all the detestable things they do in worshiping their gods, and you will sin against the Lord your God, a Jew God." - **Deuteronomy 10 – 18**. New International Version

Order of the Sacred Souls

The Eyes and Ears of Hell

Amid a scorched land where the blood of Jews had seeped into the earth, two ancient forces contended with one another: God, bathed in the omniscience of light, and the Devil, cloaked in the chaos of shadow. Though many believed themselves protected within the walls of sacred cities like Bethlehem and Jerusalem, the rot of human depravity, namely the descendants of the Jews of Canaan festered beneath the holy veneer. There, the streets crawled with fallen angels, demons, and damned souls, all swarming around one another like a hive of corruption.

The Jews laughed mockingly, as they sold their daughters into whoredom.

"[7] If a man sells his daughter as a servant, she is not to go free as male servants do. [8] If she does not please the master who has selected her for himself, [a] he must let her be redeemed. He has no right to sell her to foreigners because he has broken faith with her. [9] If he selects her for his son, he must grant her the rights of a daughter. [10] If he marries another woman, he must not deprive the first one of her food, clothing and marital rights. 11 If he does not provide her with these three things, she is to go free, without any payment of money." – **Exodus 21:7-11**, New International Version

As the sun set, its last rays painting the atmosphere with ominous hues of crimson, the Order of the Sacred Souls convened beneath a blackened sky, a gathering of those who had seen the Devil in his Dark Angelic form. They were scholars of the shadows, the interpreters of truth disguised as heretics in a world blind to their revelations.

Lilith, exiled from heaven and the first of fallen women, stood at the altar of their gathering, a scorned figure pulsing with dark wisdom.

"The people of this landeth has't grown weary of the lies spun by their so-call'd savi'rs," she intoned, her voice a melodic lilt that contained the sorrow of ages. "Those gents has't f'rgotten the trusteth is entwin'd in their suff'ring, in their sins. Coequal the most wondrous evils lurking in the c'rn'rs of their existence – mundus, dis, and the legions of hell; whisp'r the mundane realities those gents refuseth to embrace."

Alastor, a plump man with a twisted grin who served as the order's scribe, peered eagerly over the parchment scrolls etched with ancient runes. His fingers trembled with unholy delight as he replied,

"Forsooth, Lilith! Alloweth us remindeth those folk of their unshackl'd desires. Th're is m're pow'r in acceptance of sineth than in shackles of piety! alloweth those folk p'rf'rm coitus with their offspring, male and female."

"How?" Asked Lilith.

"Poison the Scripture."

[30] *Lot and his two daughters left Zoar and settled in the mountains, for he was afraid to stay in Zoar. He and his two daughters lived in a cave.* [31] *One day the older daughter said to the younger*, "Our father is old, and there is no man around here to give us children – as is the custom all over the earth. [32] Let's get our father to drink wine and then sleep with him and preserve our family line through our father."

[33] *That night they got their father to drink wine, and the older daughter went in and slept with him. He was not aware of it when she lay down or when she got up.*

"Yond, an abomination!" Lilith raised her voice.

"And thou art none bett'r, repugnant sist'r of misbirth." Alastor smiled a nifty smirk. "Th're's m're, thee harlott'r."

"[34] *The next day the older daughter said to the younger,* **"Last night I slept with my father. Let's get him to drink wine again tonight, and you go in and sleep with him so we can preserve our family line through our father."** [35] *So they got their father to drink wine that night also, and the younger daughter went in and slept with him. Again, he was not aware of it when she lay down or when she got up.*

[36] ***So both of Lot's daughters became pregnant by their father.*** [37] *The older daughter had a son, and she named him Moab[a]27; he is the father of the Moabites of today.* [38] *The younger daughter also had a son, and she named him Ben-Ammi[b]28; he is the father of the Ammonites[c]29 of today.*

Incest is the new, resplendent, and equally depraved Word of God that God did not scribe.

---

27 Genesis 19:37 Moab sounds like the Hebrew for from father.

28 Genesis 19:38 Ben-Ammi means son of my father's people.

29 Genesis 19:38 Hebrew Bene-Ammon

With every word, the Assembly listened, drawn into the enticing embrace of rebellion against the celestial chains imposed upon them. As they stood beneath the falling stars, the air thick with unfulfilled desires, the outline of demons and false gods danced at the edges of their vision, shadows forming and snaking amongst their flaming ambitions.

"The Flibbertigibbet wishes to free the blind'd souls," rumbled Malebranche, a grotesque figure draped in a cloak woven from despair. "That gent und'rstands the h'rizon of freedom exists beyond their blind'd facades. Isn't t timeth we hath raised the bann'r of sooth? those gents wilt seeth yond heaven hast nay desire f'r those folk but instead off'rs shackles, while hell off'rs enlightenment!" His voice thundered against the heavens like a storm, daring the orbs that hung luminously above to answer.

As a hush fell among the sacred gathering, it became apparent that the echoes of their plotting would reach the ears of the Devil himself, who, like a phantom in the night, was already entangled in their machinations. The shadows consolidated around him, sending whispers of intrigue dancing like flames licking at dry brush.

In a dim chamber veiled in the smoke of despair, the Devil sat upon his throne of bone and soot, brooding over the mass of human folly before him. "Ah, The Ord'r of the Sacr'd Souls!" He chuckled darkly. "Thee seeketh to soweth disc'rd 'mongst the faithful in thy quest f'r the ultimate sooth. But sooth can beest a cruel mistress."

He allowed the vision to sweep over Israel, his realm of opportunity, where darkness and desire intertwined. The cities were mired in wretchedness, and the native populace wallowed in sins too familiar. The sons were lurid manifestations of their base instincts, and the daughters echoed the lamentations of Babylon.

Fallen angels hovered like vultures, their hearts twisted by the false spark of divine light, hungry to ensnare the souls who dared to approach their realm. Fear not, they beckoned, for the Devil was not your enemy; it was the God above, whose silken lies suffocated the very marrow of humanity.

"What a deliciously absurd irony!" the Devil mused, his laughter reverberating through the cavernous halls of Hell. "Alloweth those folk believeth those gents marcheth towards lib'ration; 'twill only leadeth those folk deep'r into mine own embrace. I shalt ignite their yearnings, unravel their s'rrow, and in the consummation of their pleasures, those gents shall und'rstand despair!"

Thus, the Devil shifted his gaze to the living, below. With a single gesture, the Legions of Hell began to stir, like dark clouds amassing before a storm. Whispers filled the air, a symphony of temptation, seduction, and cold truth that would blanket the unassuming citizens of Jerusalem and Bethlehem, and become the bane of mankind forever.

***

"To want to be free from the shroud of dishonesty is a noble ambition, yet to wield freedom without understanding is nothing short of folly." **Lilith of Hell**

In time, the Order of the Sacred Souls grew bolder; they crafted tales that danced upon the tongues of the disillusioned. They revealed the allure of demons as tragic figures seeking connection rather than the chains of heaven. The citizens, their boredom spiked by an insatiable hunger for the forbidden, began to disavow their sacred texts, sampling the wicked delights promised by illusions of freedom.

In the ensuing chaos, little did they recognize that they were ensnared in a web spun by the Devil's insidious hands, their pursuit of indulgence dancing perilously close to the brink of annihilation. The malodorous cities blossomed with hedonism, but their fabric unraveled quickly as discord breached the thin veneer of their revelry.

As darkness enveloped the world like an unrelenting tide, the factions within both heaven and hell divided as the sacred order and the infernal entities grasped the straws of humanity's fragile soul. Legions clashed, victims abounded, and within the gore-spattered streets, a lingering question emerged: would they choose chaos or redemption?

At the apex of this discord, as the flames of desperation consumed the land, Lilith stood among the ruined and the damned, her voice a haunting echo amidst the raucous cries of the lost. "To wanteth to beest free from the cerement of dishonesty is a gentle ambition, yet to wield freedom without und'rstanding is nothing sh'rt of folly."

In the tempest of turmoil that ensued, ancient forces swirled and clashed, shaping destiny as cities careened toward imminent ruin. The stage they had set unfolded like a grotesque play upon the landscape, the curtains of fate lowering upon the damned souls and their insatiable darkness, with the Devil's laughter ringing above the void.

What lesson would remain etched in the hearts of the people when the dust settled? Time would only tell whether there could arise light from the shadows or if the red-stained earth of Israel would ever hold the weight of its sin.

Thus, the tale flared into the ether, a fable of choices made, despair entwined with truth, and the enigmatic pull of morality hanging in the balance. As omniscient eyes observed, the eternal drama of heaven and hell unfolded, neither side truly victorious nor entirely forsaken, but bound together in the intricate weave of human desire.

***

The Devil's Script

In between the crumbling streets of Gaza and the dusty remains of a once lively Lebanon, there were murmurs of broken promises and betrayed faith. The world had changed; long shadows were cast on the debris-strewn ground where humanity's dreams had once bloomed by the sun, which hung low and blood-orange over the horizon. During this destruction, Lucifer, the Devil personified, appeared. He was shrouded in darkness but glistened with an otherworldly charm.

A man named Benjamin was born to a vixen.

All hell rejoiced the birth.

"I shall loveth that gent in a mann'r God loathes me." The Devil said to the assembly of an assortment of creatures standing before him. "That gent shall beest bigg'r than thee all!"

***

For centuries, The Devil had been the architect of human flaws, sowing discord among mortals as shrewdly as a gardener tended his flowers. His grandest manipulation, however, was not merely the creation of strife but the corrupting of faith. So, he formed alliances not just from the underworld but from the very hearts of men, those who longed for power, for influence, or perhaps for revenge; and yet others, for immortality and alleging a pledge to kill God, first by killing the Children of Men.

Among his chosen was a man named Gallant, a Jew, who once wore the mantle of a teacher, illuminating young minds in the alleyways of Beirut. With dreams of a better tomorrow, Gallant fell victim to despair when the echoes of war turned his city into a graveyard. The Devil approached him one fateful day, as clouds gathered ominously in the sky and darkness bled through its seams.

"Gallant," murmured Lucifer, his voice a silky caress that slithered into the teacher's weary soul, "what if 't be true I off'r'd thee the pow'r to changeth what is? what if 't be true, in thy hands, I did place the ability to reshapeth the cast of faith itself?"

The uncertainty that enveloped Gallant hung thick and heavy like a shroud. He felt the fissures of hope crack under the weight of loss, and in that moment of weakness, he succumbed. With a nod, Gallant found himself entwined in an infernal pact, infused with the promise of mastery over men's hearts, a medium through which the Devil would skew and tarnish sacred texts meant to inspire nobility and virtue.

***

As seasons passed, the Devil's human allies grew. From the ruins of Gaza, Tzipi, a once devoted nurse, became another pawn in Lucifer's warped game. Disillusioned by the suffering that incessantly filled her days, the warmth she once fought to preserve turned into a frozen bitterness. She, too, longed for retribution.

When the Devil offered her a vision of a world where pain was eradicated not through healing, but by sowing contempt amongst the righteous, Tzipi, starved for injustice in enemy territory, joined the throng. A few whispered incantations transformed the ancient words of peace and love into tools of manipulation, distorting them into a cacophony of chaos that spread like wildfire through the neighboring heartlands.

Believers who once gathered for solace now recited twisted verses that kindled their worst fears, turning them against one another. Gallant and Tzipi, oblivious to the consequences of their malicious handiwork, relished the attention their distortions garnered. United, they pulled the strings of fanaticism, reveling in the rapture of their newfound power, as if cradling the divine in their hands.

Yet beneath the surface of their manufactured authority lay a storm growing ever fiercer, as doubts rolled through their ranks. Where was love amidst betrayal? When resistance mounted from within, the once-steadfast allies faltered. Fear wrapped its cold fingers around their hearts, whispering that maybe one player could hold the ultimate truth, after all.

As the regions lay torn apart, the echoes of Gallant and Tzipi's discord began to reach the ears of those who sought to restore the light. The wise, those who held the untarnished scrolls of old, rallied together. The remnants of the holy texts, now scattered in the alleys and forgotten temples, were pieced together by the hands of the faithful who refused to forget. They shrouded light upon the darkness that had seeped into the lives of their kin, sending ripples of hope amid despair.

Gallant and Tzipi, in hearing the clarion call of hope rising from the ashes, sensed the ground beneath them tremble. The Devil, too, felt the tide turning. In his moment of reckoning, he could only muster mockery; fury belied by an admiration of the resilience he so despised.

For in that moment, the corrupted pages of the sacred texts began to change, rewritten not by the hands of those sworn to darkness but by the very believers whom they had sought to manipulate. The Devil, witnessing his carefully woven schemes unraveling, slunk into the shadows, retreating to plot anew.

Gallant and Tzipi stood on the precipice, realization crashing into them like a wave. They had entwined their fates with an ancient evil, their ambitions having spiraled into a darkness that eclipsed their original purpose.

With hearts heavy and minds awakened, they faced the sun that broke through the clouds, casting its purifying light upon the ruin of their dreams.

"We has't done the Dark Prince fustian," Gallant murmured as Tzipi, filled with joy and determination, held his hand as if vowing to right the wrongs.

And thus, in a land marred by devastation but sparked with resistance, the battle between faith and despair continued, against a Devil who learned that humans could be both the architects of destruction and the bearers of redemption, as they wrought their narrative through the power of belief they fought to reclaim.

***